The Ghost's Companion

The
Ghost's Companion

A HAUNTING ANTHOLOGY

edited by
PETER HAINING

Taplinger Publishing Company | New York

Library of Congress Catalog Card Number: 75-30227 | ISBN 0-8008-3228-0

Individual Copyrights and Acknowledgements

Grateful acknowledgement is made for permission to include the following copyright material:

"A School Story" by M. R. James. Reprinted by permission of Edward Arnold Publisher, Ltd.

"The Red Lodge" by H. R. Wakefield. From *They Return at Evening*. Copyright 1928 by D. Appleton Company; renewed 1956. All rights reserved. Reprinted by permission of Hawthorn Books, Inc.

"A Haunted Island" by Algernon Blackwood. From *The Empty House*. Published in the United States by E. P. Dutton & Co., Inc., and reprinted by their permission.

"My Own True Ghost Story" by Rudyard Kipling. Reprinted by permission of Macmillan and Co., Ltd.

"The Monstrance" by Arthur Machen. Reprinted by permission of The Estate of Arthur Machen.

"Escort" by Daphne du Maurier. Reprinted by permission of the author and Curtis Brown, Ltd.

"South Sea Bubble" by Hammond Innes. Reprinted by permission of *Punch* magazine.

"Hallowe'en for Mr. Faulkner" by August Derleth. Copyright © 1959 by Great American Publications, Inc., for *Fantastic Universe*, November 1959. Reprinted by permission of Arkham House Publishers, Inc.

"The Ghost" by Richard Hughes. First published in *A Moment in Time*. Copyright 1926 by Richard Hughes; renewed 1954. Reprinted by permission of Harold Ober Agency.

"The Case of the Red-Headed Women" by Dennis Wheatley. From *Gunmen, Gallants, and Ghosts*. Copyright 1943 by Dennis Wheatley. Reprinted by permission of the author and Hutchinson Publishers Group, Ltd.

"Smoke Ghost" by Fritz Leiber. Reprinted by permission of E. J. Carnell Agency.

"Aunt Jezebel's House" by Joan Aiken. Reprinted by permission of the author.

"Fever Dream" by Ray Bradbury. From *A Medicine for Melancholy*. Copyright © 1959 by Ray Bradbury. Reprinted by permission of Harold Matson Company, Inc.

The editor also wishes to thank Mrs. Joanna Goldsworthy of Victor Gollancz Ltd. for her enthusiasm for this project and ensuring that the right "spirits" were put into the book.

For

DENIS GIFFORD

—who knows a good ghost
story when he sees one

Contents

Editor's Introduction

THERE have been many books about ghosts, of course. A great number of them are by people most conveniently described as 'professional' ghost hunters: men, and a few women, too, who have industriously pursued the supernatural in many parts of the world, investigating both ancient legends and modern encounters. Their reports, mainly based on first-hand experience or else on the most carefully authenticated eye-witness stories, have provided a wealth of material of great importance in the continuing study of this phenomenon—perhaps the oldest known to mankind.

An off-shoot of this research has been the ghost story—a blending of the various elements of a haunting with the storyteller's art. It is undoubtedly one of the most attractive themes for writers of macabre fiction, and indeed modern exponents are only continuing a tradition which dates back to the times of the Ancient Egyptians. As Dr Peter Penzoldt has remarked in his book, *The Supernatural in Fiction* (1950), 'The ghost is the most constant figure in supernatural fiction. It appears from the beginning of literature. In the first book of Samuel we find the story about the Witch of Endor, and in Homer's "Odyssey" the hero goes to visit the shades of Hades.'

The phantom has become an integral and accepted part of our lives. In Britain, for instance, no Christmas season is quite complete without a ghost story or two, and in America a whole day each year is given over to the ghost and his fellow denizens of the dark—the day of Hallowe'en. Elsewhere, in Europe, India, the Far East, and just about anywhere you care to name, similar ghostly traditions will be found every bit as varied and steeped in mystery. All this is grist to the ghost story writer's mill.

What, however, few of the multitudinous books on ghosts have done is to bring together famous authors—not necessarily those specialising in the supernatural and the macabre —who have actually come face to face with a phantom and subsequently turned their experience into a story. In a sentence, that is what this collection has attempted.

Perhaps surprisingly, my researches in supernatural literature have shown that such encounters are by no means as infrequent as one might expect. One would think that the majority of authors, who are on the whole sceptical and objective, would have found some explanation for what had happened to them; and that if they used their experience in their work, they would present it in a wholly impersonal way. Instead, they have examined and reappraised their experience and found it convincing enough to be put forward openly for the examination of the public.

To attempt to present even a cross-section of such stories arising from over 2,000 years of literature would, quite obviously, be impossible, and consequently I have taken as my guideline Professor Penzoldt's statement that, 'Although the short ghost story became a popular form in English literature during the nineteenth century, it only attained its present degree of perfection in the past fifty years.' This, therefore, is a book of ghost stories from the twentieth century only. I also believe that there are far too many collections filled with all the old stories of ghosts in white shrouds, moaning in sorrow and rattling in their chains.

Today's reader, I think, deserves more up-to-date fare: the ghost as he (or she) is seen and experienced today. So here you will find no stories of 'something happening' but rather some of the best tales of ingenuity, atmosphere, and perhaps most important of all, believability.

I have begun the book, naturally enough, perhaps, with a contribution by M. R. James, arguably the greatest of all ghost story writers. It was he who ushered the genre into this century with a series of unique and compelling tales which have been the envy of all writers and the models for any author who would tackle such stories. As a comparatively new professor, Dr James experienced a strange brush with the unknown which both influenced and inspired his work, as the opening story in our collection shows, and so it was to varying degrees with all our other contributors.

In my introduction to each story I have included brief details of the 'haunting' which inspired the author, thereby giving an added piquancy to what follows. It has been fascinating, not to say surprising, to learn the facts behind the ghostly fiction, and I trust that you, too, will now enjoy being in the company of phantoms for a few hours.

PETER HAINING

The Ghost's Companion

A School Story

M. R. JAMES

Perhaps, like me, you heard your first ghost story at school. It is not unlikely, because we all have a desire to frighten each other from time to time, and the telling of tales about 'things that go bump in the night' comes upon us early in life. Where else, then, would it be more appropriate to start such a collection as this than in a school and in the company of the professor whose very name is synonymous with ghosts stories, Dr Montague Rhodes James. Dr James, who devoted his life to academic pursuits and was for many years the Provost of Eton, believed implicitly in ghosts as he demonstrated in his remarkable stories. What few of his readers knew was that he had actually had a brush with the supernatural early in his own life. It happened in 1884 when he was studying at King's College, Cambridge, and lived in Gibbs Buildings. The atmosphere of the whole place was strange, he remembered, and it was made more so by an old man who lived in rooms nearby and kept a coffin beside his bed! 'There were grim stories told about him,' Dr James recalled, 'the grimmest of which are too grim to set down.' The building was also said to be haunted. 'Ghosts and ghostly phenomena are rare in colleges,' Dr James noted in his biography years later, 'and highly suspect when they do occur. Yet, on the staircase next to mine was a ghostly cry in the bedroom. Other professors knew of it, and knew whose voice it was believed to be—of a man who died in 1878.' It was the remembrance of this experience which he embodied into "A School Story".

Two men in a smoking-room were talking of their private-school days. 'At *our* school,' said A., 'we had a ghost's foot-mark on the staircase. What was it like? Oh, very unconvincing. Just the shape of a shoe, with a square toe, if I remember right. The staircase was a stone one. I never heard any story about the thing. That seems odd, when you come to think of it. Why didn't somebody invent one, I wonder?'

'You never can tell with little boys. They have a mythology of their own. There's a subject for you, by the way— "The Folklore of Private Schools" '.

'Yes; the crop is rather scanty, though. I imagine, if you were to investigate the cycle of ghost stories, for instance, which the boys at private schools tell each other, they would all turn out to be highly-compressed versions of stories out of books.'

'Nowadays the *Strand* and *Pearson's*, and so on, would be extensively drawn upon.'

'No doubt: they weren't born or thought of in *my* time. Let's see. I wonder if I can remember the staple ones that I was told. First, there was the house with a room in which a series of people insisted on passing a night; and each of them in the morning was found kneeling in a corner, and had just time to say, "I've seen it," and died.'

'Wasn't that the house in Berkeley Square?'

'I dare say it was. Then there was the man who heard a noise in the passage at night, opened his door, and saw someone crawling towards him on all fours with his eye hanging out on his cheek. There was besides, let me think—— Yes! the room where a man was found dead in bed with a horseshoe mark on his forehead, and the floor under the bed was covered with marks of horseshoes also; I don't know why. Also there was the lady who, on locking her bedroom door in a strange house, heard a thin voice among the bed-curtains say, "Now we're shut in for the night." None of those had any explanation or sequel. I wonder if they go on still, those stories.'

'Oh, likely enough—with additions from the magazines, as I said. You never heard, did you, of a real ghost at a private school? I thought not; nobody has that ever I came across.'

'From the way in which you said that, I gather that *you* have.'

'I really don't know; but this is what was in my mind. It happened at my private school thirty-odd years ago, and I haven't any explanation of it.

'The school I mean was near London. It was established in a large and fairly old house—a great white building with very fine grounds about it; there were large cedars in the garden, as there are in so many of the older gardens in the Thames valley, and ancient elms in the three or four fields which we used for our games. I think probably it was quite an attractive place, but boys seldom allow that their schools possess any tolerable features.

'I came to the school in a September, soon after the year 1870; and among the boys who arrived on the same day was one whom I took to: a Highland boy, whom I will call McLeod. I needn't spend time in describing him: the main thing is that I got to know him very well. He was not an exceptional boy in any way—not particularly good at books or games—but he suited me.

'The school was a large one: there must have been from 120 to 130 boys there as a rule, and so a considerable staff of masters was required, and there were rather frequent changes among them.

'One term—perhaps it was my third or fourth—a new master made his appearance. His name was Sampson. He was a tallish, stoutish, pale, black-bearded man. I think we liked him: he had travelled a good deal, and had stories which amused us on our school walks, so that there was some competition among us to get within earshot of him. I remember too—dear me, I have hardly thought of it since then!—that he had a charm on his watch-chain that attracted my attention one day, and he let me examine it. It was, I now suppose, a gold Byzantine coin; there was an effigy of some absurd emperor on one side; the other side had been worn practically smooth, and he had had cut on it —rather barbarously—his own initials, G.W.S., and a date, 24 July, 1865. Yes, I can see it now: he told me he had picked it up in Constantinople: it was about the size of a florin, perhaps rather smaller.

'Well, the first odd thing that happened was this. Sampson was doing Latin grammar with us. One of his favourite methods—perhaps it is rather a good one—was to make us construct sentences out of our own heads to illustrate the rules he was trying to make us learn. Of course that is a thing which gives a silly boy a chance of being impertinent: there are lots of school stories in which that happens—or anyhow there might be. But Sampson was too good a disciplinarian for us to think of trying that one with him. Now, on this occasion he was telling us how to express *remembering* in Latin: and he ordered us each to make a sentence bringing the verb *memini*, "I remember." Well, most of us made up some ordinary sentence such as "I remember my father," or "He remembers his book," or something equally uninteresting: and I dare say a good many put down *memino librum meum*, and so forth: but the boy I mentioned—McLeod—was evidently thinking of something more elaborate than that. The rest of us wanted to have our sentences passed, and get on to something else, so some kicked him under the desk, and I, who was next to him, poked him and whispered to him to look sharp. But he didn't seem to attend. I looked at his paper and saw he had put down nothing at all. So I jogged him again harder than before and upbraided him sharply for keeping us all waiting. That did have some effect. He started and seemed to wake up, and then very quickly he scribbled about a couple of lines on his paper, and showed it up with the rest. As it was the last, or nearly the last, to come in, and as Sampson had a good deal to say to the boys who had written *meminiscimus patri meo* and the rest of it, it turned out that the clock struck twelve before he had got to McLeod, and McLeod had to wait afterwards to have his sentence corrected. There was nothing much going on outside when I got out, so I waited for him to come. He came very slowly when he did arrive, and I guessed there had been some sort of trouble. "Well," I said, "what did you get?" "Oh, I don't know," said McLeod, "nothing much: but I think Sampson's rather sick with me." "Why, did you show him up some rot?" "No fear," he said. "It was all right as far as I could see: it was like this. *Memento*—that's right enough for remember, and it takes a genitive,—*memento putei inter quatuor taxos.*" "What silly rot!" I said. "What made you shove that down? What does it mean?" "That's the funny part," said McLeod. "I'm not quite sure what it does mean. All I know is, it just came into my head and I corked it down. I know what I *think* it means, because just before I wrote it down I had a sort of picture of it in my head: I believe it means 'Remember the well among the four'—what are those dark sort of trees that have red berries on them?" "Mountain

ashes, I s'pose you mean." "I never heard of them," said
McLeod; "no, *I'll* tell you—yews." "Well, and what did
Sampson say?" "Why, he was jolly odd about it. When he
read it he got up and went to the mantelpiece and stopped
quite a long time without saying anything, with his back to
me. And then he said, without turning round, and rather
quiet, 'What do you suppose that means?' I told him what I
thought; only I couldn't remember the name of the silly
tree: and then he wanted to know why I put it down,
and I had to say something or other. And after that
he left off talking about it, and asked me how long I'd
been here, and where my people lived, and things like
that: and then I came away: but he wasn't looking a bit
well."

'I don't remember any more that was said by either of us
about this. Next day McLeod took to his bed with a chill or
something of the kind, and it was a week or more before he
was in school again. And as much as a month went by without anything happening that was noticeable. Whether or not
Mr Sampson was really startled, as McLeod had thought,
he didn't show it. I am pretty sure, of course, now, that there
was something very curious in his past history, but I'm not
going to pretend that we boys were sharp enough to guess
any such thing.

'There was one other incident of the same kind as the last
which I told you. Several times since that day we had had
to make up examples in school to illustrate different rules,
but there had never been any row except when we did them
wrong. At last there came a day when we were going
through those dismal things which people call Conditional
Sentences, and we were told to make a conditional sentence,
expressing a future consequence. We did it, right or wrong,
and showed up our bits of paper, and Sampson began looking through them. All at once he got up, made some odd
sort of noise in his throat, and rushed out by a door that was
just by his desk. We sat there for a minute or two, and then—

I suppose it was incorrect—but we went up, I and one or two others, to look at the papers on his desk. Of course I thought someone must have put down some nonsense or other, and Sampson had gone off to report him. All the same, I noticed that he hadn't taken any of the papers with him when he ran out. Well, the top paper on the desk was written in red ink—which no one used—and it wasn't in anyone's hand who was in the class. They all looked at it— McLeod and all—and took their dying oaths that it wasn't theirs. Then I thought of counting the bits of paper. And of this I made quite certain: that there were seventeen bits of paper on the desk, and sixteen boys in the form. Well, I bagged the extra paper, and kept it, and I believe I have it now. And now you will want to know what was written on it. It was simple enough, and harmless enough, I should have said.

' "*Si tu non veneris ad me, ego veniam ad te,*"
which means, I suppose, "If you don't come to me, I'll come to you." ' '

'Could you show me the paper?' interrupted the listener.

'Yes, I could: but there's another odd thing about it. That same afternoon I took it out of my locker—I know for certain it was the same bit, for I made a finger-mark on it— and no single trace of writing of any kind was there on it. I kept it, as I said, and since that time I have tried various experiments to see whether sympathetic ink had been used, but absolutely without result.

'So much for that. After about half an hour Sampson looked in again: said he had felt very unwell, and told us we might go. He came rather gingerly to his desk, and gave just one look at the uppermost paper: and I suppose he thought he must have been dreaming: anyhow, he asked no questions.

'That day was a half-holiday, and next day Sampson was in school again, much as usual. That night the third and last incident in my story happened.

'We—McLeod and I—slept in a dormitory at right angles
to the main building. Sampson slept in the main building on
the first floor. There was a very bright full moon. At an hour
which I can't tell exactly, but some time between one and
two, I was woken up by somebody shaking me. It was
McLeod; and a nice state of mind he seemed to be in.
"Come," he said,—"come! there's a burglar getting in
through Sampson's window." As soon as I could speak, I
said, "Well, why not call out and wake everybody up?"
"No, no," he said, "I'm not sure who it is: don't make a
row: come and look." Naturally I came and looked, and
naturally there was no one there. I was cross enough, and
should have called McLeod plenty of names: only—I
couldn't tell why—it seemed to me that there *was* something
wrong—something that made me very glad I wasn't alone to
face it. We were still at the window looking out, and as soon
as I could, I asked him what he had heard or seen. "I didn't
hear anything at all," he said, "but about five minutes before
I woke you, I found myself looking out of this window here,
and there was a man sitting or kneeling on Sampson's
window-sill, and looking in, and I thought he was beckon-
ing." "What sort of man?" McLeod wriggled. "I don't
know," he said, "but I can tell you one thing—he was
beastly thin: and he looked as if he was wet all over: and,"
he said, looking round and whispering as if he hardly
liked to hear himself, "I'm not at all sure that he was
alive."

'We went on talking in whispers some time longer, and
eventually crept back to bed. No one else in the room woke
or stirred the whole time. I believe we did sleep a bit afterwards, but we were very cheap next day.

'And next day Mr Sampson was gone: not to be found:
and I believe no trace of him has ever come to light since. In
thinking it over, one of the oddest things about it all has
seemed to me to be the fact that neither McLeod nor I
ever mentioned what we had seen to any third person

whatever. Of course no questions were asked on the subject, and if they had been, I am inclined to believe that we could not have made any answer: we seemed unable to speak about it.

'That is my story,' said the narrator. 'The only approach to a ghost story connected with a school that I know, but still, I think, an approach to such a thing.'

The sequel to this may perhaps be reckoned highly conventional; but a sequel there is, and so it must be produced. There had been more than one listener to the story, and, in the latter part of that same year, or of the next, one such listener was staying at a country house in Ireland.

One evening his host was turning over a drawer full of odds and ends in the smoking-room. Suddenly he put his hand upon a little box. 'Now,' he said, 'you know about old things; tell me what that is.' My friend opened the little box, and found in it a thin gold chain with an object attached to it. He glanced at the object and then took off his spectacles to examine it more narrowly. 'What's the history of this?' he asked. 'Odd enough,' was the answer. 'You know the yew thicket in the shrubbery: well, a year or two back we were cleaning out the old well that used to be in the clearing here, and what do you suppose we found?'

'Is it possible that you found a body?' said the visitor, with an odd feeling of nervousness.

'We did that: but what's more, in every sense of the word, we found two.'

'Good Heavens! Two? Was there anything to show how they got there? Was this thing found with them?'

'It was. Amongst the rags of the clothes that were on one of the bodies. A bad business, whatever the story of it may have been. One body had the arms tight round the other. They must have been there thirty years or more—long enough before we came to this place. You may judge we

filled the well up fast enough. Do you make anything of
what's cut on that gold coin you have there?'

'I think I can,' said my friend, holding it to the light
(but he read it without much difficulty); 'it seems to be
G.W.S., 24 July, 1865.'

The Red Lodge

H. R. WAKEFIELD

The great majority of ghosts are associated with a building of some kind, as the most widely held theory about their existence is that they are the spirits of people who once dwelt on the premises. The Haunted House, particularly, is a constantly recurring subject in factual reports of ghosts and probably wherever the reader happens to pick up this book there will be a place somewhere in the vicinity with just such a reputation. Naturally, the theme has attracted many writers of supernatural stories, but I doubt that there has been a more vivid tale than H. R. Wakefield's "The Red Lodge" which, the author has revealed, was based on events at a Queen Anne house he lived in near Richmond Bridge. Although critics have compared his work to that of Joseph Sheridan Le Fanu and M. R.

James, Wakefield is rather neglected today and it is a pleasure to bring him back into print with this particular story of which he has written, 'I first visited the Richmond house in 1917 and during the previous thirty years it had known five suicides, and others had drowned themselves in the river about a hundred yards away, always at dawn. The valet of a famous nobleman was seen running down the path as though a fearful fiend was hard upon his heels and plunged in to his death. . . . The house always seemed unnaturally dim, and the moment I passed its threshold I knew a general feeling of devitalisation and general psychic malaise which remained until I left. I was sitting in the garden one afternoon under the mulberry tree and happened to glance up at the first floor windows. There was a blurred face at one of them. It was a man's face, but there was no man in the house. I wrote my first story about that house and called it "The Red Lodge".'

I am writing this from an imperative sense of duty, for I consider the Red Lodge is a foul death-trap and utterly unfit to be a human habitation—it has its own proper denizens—and because I know its owner to be an unspeakable black-guard to allow it so to be used for his financial advantage. He knows the perils of the place perfectly well; I wrote to him of our experiences, and he didn't even acknowledge the letter, and two days ago I saw the ghastly pest-house advertised in *Country Life*. So anyone who rents the Red Lodge in future will receive a copy of this document as well as some uncomfortable words from Sir William and that scoundrel Wilkes can take what action he pleases.

I certainly didn't carry any prejudice against the place down to it with me: I had been too busy to look over it myself, but my wife reported extremely favourably—I take her word for most things—and I could tell by the photographs that it was a magnificent specimen of the medium-sized Queen Anne house, just the ideal thing for me. Mary said the garden was perfect, and there was the river for Tim at the bottom of it. I had been longing for a holiday,

and was in the highest spirits as I travelled down. I have
not been in the highest spirits since.

My first vague, faint uncertainty came to me as soon as I
had crossed the threshold. I am a painter by profession, and
therefore sharply responsive to colour tone. Well, it was a
brilliantly fine day, the hall of the Red Lodge was fully lit,
yet it seemed a shade off the key, as it were, as though I
were regarding it through a pair of slightly darkened glasses.
Only a painter would have noticed it, I fancy.

When Mary came out to greet me, she was not looking as
well as I had hoped, or as well as a week in the country
should have made her look.

'Everything all right?' I asked.

'Oh, yes,' she replied, but I thought she found it difficult
to say so, and then my eye detected a curious little spot of
green on the maroon rug in front of the fire-place. I picked
it up—it seemed like a patch of river slime.

'I suppose Tim brings those in,' said Mary. 'I've found
several; of course, he promises he doesn't.' And then for a
moment we were silent, and a very unusual sense of con-
straint seemed to set a barrier between us. I went out into
the garden to smoke a cigarette before lunch, and sat
myself down under a very fine mulberry tree.

I wondered if, after all, I had been wise to have left it all
to Mary. There was nothing wrong with the house, or
course, but I am a bit psychic, and I always know the mood
or character of a house. One welcomes you with the tail-
writhing enthusiasm of a really nice dog, makes you at
home, and at your ease at once. Others are sullen, watchful,
hostile, with things to hide. They make you feel that you
have obtruded yourself into some curious affairs which are
none of your business. I had never encountered so hostile,
aloof, and secretive a living place as the Red Lodge seemed
when I first entered it. Well, it couldn't be helped, though
it was disappointing; and there was Tim coming back from
his walk, and the luncheon-gong. My son seemed a little

subdued and thoughtful, though he looked pretty well, and
soon we were all chattering away with those quick changes
of key which occur when the respective ages of the con-
versationalists are 40, 33 and 6½, and after half a bottle of
Meursault and a glass of port I began to think I had been
a morbid ass. I was still so thinking when I began my holiday in the best possible way by going to sleep in an exquisitely
comfortable chair under the mulberry tree. But I have
slept better. I dozed off, but I had a silly impression of being
watched, so that I kept waking up in case there might be
someone with his eye on me. I was lying back, and could
just see a window on the second floor framed by a gap in
the leaves, and on one occasion, when I woke rather sharply
from one of these dozes, I thought I saw for a moment a
face peering down at me and this face seemed curiously
flattened against the pane—just a 'carry over' from a
dream, I concluded. However, I didn't feel like sleeping
any more, and began to explore the garden. It was completely walled in, I found, except at the far end, where
there was a door leading through to a path which, running
parallel to the right-hand wall, led to the river a few yards
away. I noticed on this door several of those patches of green
slime for which Tim was supposedly responsible. It was a
dark little corner cut off from the rest of the garden by two
rowan trees, a cool silent little place I thought it. And then
it was time for Tim's cricket lesson, which was interrupted
by the arrival of some infernal callers. But they were pleasant
people, as a matter of fact, the Local Knuts, I gathered,
who owned the Manor House: Sir William Prowse and his
lady and his daughter. I went for a walk with him after tea.

'Who had this house before us?' I asked.

'People called Hawker,' he replied. 'That was two years
ago.'

'I wonder the owner doesn't live in it,' I said. 'It isn't an
expensive place to keep up.'

Sir William paused as if considering his reply.

'I think he dislikes being so near the river. I'm not sorry, for I detest the fellow. By the way, how long have you taken it for?'

'Three months,' I replied, 'till the end of October.'

'Well, if I can do anything for you I shall be delighted. If you are in any trouble, come straight to me.' He slightly emphasised the last sentence.

I rather wondered what sort of trouble Sir William envisaged for me. Probably he shared the general opinion that artists were quite mad at times, and that when I had one of my lapses I should destroy the peace in some manner. However, I was duly grateful.

I was sorry to find Tim didn't seem to like the river; he appeared nervous of it, and I determined to help him to overcome this, for the fewer terrors one carries through life with one the better, and they can often be laid by delicate treatment in childhood. Curiously enough the year before at Frinton he seemed to have no fear of the sea.

The rest of the day passed uneventfully—at least I think I can say so. After dinner I strolled down to the end of the garden, meaning to go through the door and have a look at the river. Just as I got my hand on the latch there came a very sharp, furtive whistle. I turned round quickly, but seeing no one, concluded it had come from someone in the lane outside. However, I didn't investigate further, but went back to the house.

I woke up the next morning feeling a shade depressed. My dressing-room smelled stale and bitter, and I flung its windows open. As I did so I felt my right foot slip on something. It was one of those small, slimy, green patches. Now Tim would never come into my dressing-room. An annoying little puzzle. How on earth had that patch—? Which question kept forcing its way into my mind as I dressed. How could a patch of green slime . . .? How could a patch of green slime . . .? Dropped from something? From what? I am very fond of my wife—she slaved for me when I was

poor, and always has kept me happy, comfortable and
faithful, and she gave me my small son Timothy. I must
stand between her and patches of green slime! What in
hell's name was I talking about? And it was a flamingly
fine day. Yet all during breakfast my mind was trying to
find some sufficient reason for these funny little patches of
green slime, and not finding it.

After breakfast I told Tim I would take him out in a boat
on the river.

'Must I, Daddy?' he asked, looking anxiously at me.

'No, of course not,' I replied, a trifle irritably, 'but I
believe you'll enjoy it.'

'Should I be a funk if I didn't come?'

'No, Tim, but I think you should try it once, anyway.'

'All right,' he said.

He's a plucky little chap, and did his very best to pretend
to be enjoying himself, but I saw it was a failure from the
start.

Perplexed and upset, I asked his nurse if she knew of any
reason for this sudden fear of water.

'No, sir,' she said. 'The first day he ran down to the river
just as he used to run down to the sea, but all of a sudden
he started crying and ran back to the house. It seemed to
me he'd seen something in the water which frightened
him.'

We spent the afternoon motoring round the neighbourhood, and already I found a faint distaste at the idea of
returning to the house, and again I had the impression
that we were intruding, and that something had been going
on during our absence which our return had interrupted.

Mary, pleading a headache, went to bed soon after
dinner, and I went to the study to read.

Directly I had shut the door I had again that very
unpleasant sensation of being watched. It made the reading
of Sidgwick's *The Use of Words in Reasoning*—an old favourite
of mine, which requires concentration—a difficult business.

Time after time I found myself peeping into dark corners and shifting my position. And there were little sharp sounds; just the oak-panelling cracking, I supposed. After a time I became more absorbed in the book, and less fidgety, and then I heard a very soft cough just behind me. I felt little icy rays pour down and through me, but I would *not* look round, and I *would* go on reading. I had just reached the following passage: 'However many things may be said about Socrates, or about any fact observed, there remains still more that might be said if the need arose; the need is the determining factor. Hence the distinction between complete and incomplete description, though perfectly sharp and clear in the abstract, can only have a meaning—can only be applied to actual cases—if it be taken as equivalent to *sufficient* description, the sufficiency being relative to some purpose. Evidently the description of Socrates as a man, scanty though it is, may be fully sufficient for the purpose of the modest inquiry whether he is *mortal* or not'—when my eye was caught by a green patch which suddenly appeared on the floor beside me, and then another and another, following a straight line towards the door. I picked up the nearest one, and it was a bit of soaking slime. I called on all my will-power, for I feared something worse to come, and it should *not* materialise —and then no more patches appeared. I got up and walked deliberately, slowly, to the door, turned on the light in the middle of the room, and then came back and turned out the reading-lamp and went to my dressing-room. I sat down and thought things over. There was something very wrong with this house. I had passed the stage of pretending otherwise, and my inclination was to take my family away from it the next day. But that meant sacrificing £168, and we had nowhere else to go. It was conceivable that these phenomena were perceptible only to me, being half a Highlander. I might be able to stick it out if I were careful and kept my tail up, for apparitions of this sort are partially subjective—one brings something of oneself to their material-isation. That is a hard saying, but I believe it to be true. If Mary and Tim and the servants were immune it was up to me to face and fight this nastiness. As I undressed, I came to the decision that I would decide nothing then and there, and that I would see what happened. I made this decision against my better judgment, I think.

In bed I tried to thrust all this away from me by a conscious effort to 'change the subject'. as it were. The easiest subject for me to switch over to is the myriad-sided, useless, consistently abused business of creating things, stories out of pens and ink and paper, representations of things and moods out of paint, brushes and canvas, and our own miseries, perhaps, out of wine, women and song. With a considerable effort, therefore, and with the edges of my brain anxious to be busy with bits of green slime, I recalled an article I had read that day on a glorious word 'Jugend-bewegung', the 'Youth Movement', that pregnant or merely wind-swollen Teutonism! How ponderously it attempted to canonise with its polysyllabic sonority that inverted Boy-Scoutishness of the said youths and maidens. 'One bad, mad deed—sonnet—scribble of some kind—lousy daub—a day.' Bunk without spunk, sauce without force, Futurism without a past, merely a *Transition* from one yelping pose to another. And then I suddenly found myself at the end of the garden, attempting desperately to hide myself behind a rowan tree, while my eyes were held relentlessly to face the door. And then it began slowly to open, and something which was horridly unlike anything I had seen before began passing through it, and *I* knew It knew I was there, and then my head seemed burst and flamed asunder, splintered and destroyed, and I awoke trembling to feel that something in the darkness was poised an inch or two above me, and then drip, drip, drip, something began falling on my face. Mary was in the bed next to mine, and I *would not* scream, but flung the clothes over my head, my eyes streaming with the tears of terror. And so I remained cowered till I heard the clock strike five, and dawn, the ally I longed for, came, and the birds began to sing, and then I slept.

I awoke a wreck, and after breakfast, feeling the need to be alone, I pretended I wanted to sketch, and went out into the garden. Suddenly I recalled Sir William's remark about coming to see him if there was any trouble. Not much difficulty in guessing what he had meant. I'd go and see him about it at once. I wished I knew whether Mary was troubled, too. I hesitated to ask her, for, if she were not, she was certain to become suspicious and uneasy if I questioned her. And then I discovered that, while my brain had been busy with its thoughts, my hand had also not been idle, but had been occupied in drawing a very singular design on the sketching-block. I watched it as it went automatically on. Was it a design or a figure of some sort? When had I seen something like it before? My God, in my dream last night! I tore it to pieces, and got up in agitation and made my way to the Manor House along a path through tall, bowing, stippled grasses hissing lightly in the breeze. My inclination was to run to the station and take the next train to any-where; pure undiluted panic—an insufficiently analysed word—that which causes men to trample on women and children when Death is making his choice. Of course, I had Mary and Tim and the servants to keep me from it, but supposing they had no claim on me, should I desert them? No, I should not. Why? Such things aren't done by respect-able inhabitants of Great Britain—a people despised and respected by all other tribes. Despised as Philistines, but it took the jawbone of an ass to subdue that hardy race! Respected for what? Birkenhead stuff. No, not the noble Lord, for there were no glittering prizes for those who went down to the bottom of the sea in ships. My mind deliberately restricting itself to such highly debatable jingoism, I reached the Manor House, to be told that Sir William was up in London for the day, but would return that evening. Would he ring me up on his return? 'Yes, sir.' And then, with lagging steps, back to the Red Lodge.

I took Mary for a drive in the car after lunch. Anything to get out of the beastly place. Tim didn't come as he preferred to play in the garden. In the light of what happened I suppose I shall be criticised for leaving him alone with a nurse, but at that time I held the theory that these appearances were in no way malignant, and that it was more than possible that even if Tim did see anything he wouldn't be frightened, not realising it was out of the ordinary in any way. After all, nothing that I had seen or heard, at any rate during the daytime, would strike him as unusual.

Mary was very silent, and I was beginning to feel sure, from a certain depression and oppression in her manner and appearance, that my trouble was hers. It was on the tip of my tongue to say something, but I resolved to wait until I had heard what Sir William had to say. It was a dark, sombre, and brooding afternoon, and my spirits fell as we turned for home. What a home!

We got back at six, and I had just stopped the engine and helped Mary out when I heard a scream from the garden. I rushed round, to see Tim, his hands to his eyes, staggering across the lawn, the nurse running behind him. And then he screamed again and fell. I carried him into the house and laid him down on a sofa in the drawing-room, and Mary went to him. I took the nurse by the arm and out of the room; she was panting and crying down a face of chalk.

'What happened? What happened?' I asked.

'I don't know what it was, sir, but we had been walking in the lane, and had left the door open. Master Tim was a bit ahead of me, and went through the door first, and then he screamed like that.'

'Did you see anything that could have frightened him?'

'No, sir, nothing.'

I went back to them. It was no good questioning Tim, and

there was nothing coherent to be learnt from his hysterical sobbing. He grew calmer presently, and was taken up to bed. Suddenly he turned to Mary, and looked at her with eyes of terror.

'The green monkey won't get me, will it, Mummy?'

'No, no, it's all right now,' said Mary, and soon after he went to sleep, and then she and I went down to the drawing-room. She was on the border of hysteria herself.

'Oh, Tom, what is the matter with this awful house? I'm *terrified*. Ever since I've been here I've been terrified. Do you see things?'

'Yes,' I replied.

'Oh, I wish I'd known. I didn't want to worry you if you hadn't. Let me tell you what it's been like. On the day we arrived I saw a man pass ahead of me into my bedroom. Of course, I only *thought* I had. And then I've heard beastly whisperings, and every time I pass that turn in the corridor I *know* there's someone just round the corner. And then the day before you arrived I woke suddenly, and something seemed to force me to go to the window, and I crawled there on hands and knees and peeped through the blind. It was just light enough to see. And suddenly I saw someone running down the lawn, his or her hands outstretched, and there was something ghastly just beside him, and they disappeared behind the trees at the end. I'm terrified every minute.'

'What about the servants?'

'Nurse hasn't seen anything, but the others have, I'm certain. And then there are those slimy patches, I think they're the vilest of all. I don't think Tim has been troubled till now, but I'm sure he's been puzzled and uncertain several times.'

'Well,' I said, 'it's pretty obvious we must clear out. I'm seeing Sir William about it tomorrow, I hope, and I'm certain enough of what he'll advise. Meanwhile we must think over where to go. It is a nasty jar, though; I don't mean merely the money, though that's bad enough, but the fuss—just when I hoped we were going to be so happy and settled. However, it's got to be done. We should be mad after a week of this filth-drenched hole.'

Just then the telephone-bell rang. It was a message to say Sir William would be pleased to see me at half-past ten tomorrow.

With the dusk came that sense of being watched, waited for, followed about, plotted against, an atmosphere of quiet, hunting malignancy. A thick mist came up from the river, and as I was changing for dinner I noticed the lights from the windows seemed to project a series of swiftly changing pictures on its grey, crawling screen. The one opposite my window, for example, was unpleasantly suggestive of three figures staring in and seeming to grow nearer and larger. The effect must have been slightly hypnotic, for suddenly I started back, for it was as if they were about to close on me. I pulled down the blind and hurried downstairs. During dinner we decided that unless Sir William had something very reassuring to say we would go back to London two days later and stay at an hotel till we could find somewhere to spend the next six weeks. Just before going to bed we went up to the night nursery to see if Tim was all right. This room was at the top of a short flight of stairs. As these stairs were covered with green slime, and there was a pool of the muck just outside the door, we took him down to sleep with us.

The Permanent Occupants of the Red Lodge waited till the light was out, but then I felt them come thronging, slipping in one by one, their weapon fear. It seemed to me they were massed for the attack. A yard away my wife was lying with my son in her arms, so I must fight. I lay back, gripped the sides of the bed and strove with all my might to hold my assailants back. As the hours went by I felt myself beginning to get the upper hand, and a sense of exaltation came to me. But an hour before dawn they made their greatest effort. I knew that they were willing me to creep on my hands and knees to the window and peep through the blind, and that if I did so we were doomed. As I set my teeth and tightened my grip till I felt racked with agony, the sweat poured from me. I felt them come crowding round the bed and thrusting their faces into mine, and a voice in my head kept saying insistently, 'You must crawl to the window and look through the blind.' In my mind's eye I could see myself crawling stealthily across the floor and pulling the blind aside, but who would be staring back at me? Just when I felt my resistance breaking I heard a sweet, sleepy twitter from a tree outside, and saw the blind touched by a faint suggestion of light, and at once those with whom I had been struggling left me and went their way, and, utterly exhausted, I slept.

In the morning I found, somewhat ironically, that Mary had slept better than on any night since she came down.

Half-past ten found me entering the Manor House, a delightful nondescript old place, which started wagging its tail as soon as I entered it. Sir William was awaiting me in the library. 'I expected this would happen,' he said gravely, 'and now tell me.'

I gave him a short outline of our experiences.

'Yes,' he said, 'it's always much the same story. Every time that horrible place has been let I have felt a sense of personal responsibility, and yet I cannot give a proper warning, for the letting of haunted houses is not yet a criminal offence—though it ought to be—and I couldn't afford a libel action, and, as a matter of fact, one old couple had the house for fifteen years and were perfectly delighted with it, being troubled in no way. But now let me tell you what I know of the Red Lodge. I have studied it for forty years, and I regard it as my personal enemy.

'The local tradition is that the second owner, early in the eighteenth century, wished to get rid of his wife, and bribed his servants to frighten her to death—just the sort of ancestor

I can imagine that blackguard Wilkes being descended from.

'What devilries they perpetrated I don't know, but she is supposed to have rushed from the house just before dawn one day and drowned herself. Whereupon her husband installed a small harem in the house; but it was a failure, for each of these charmers one by one rushed down to the river just before dawn, and finally the husband himself did the same. Of the period between then and forty years ago I have no record, but the local tradition has it that it was the scene of tragedy after tragedy, and then was shut up for a long time. When I first began to study it, it was occupied by two bachelor brothers. One shot himself in the room which I imagine you use as your bedroom, and the other drowned himself in the usual way. I may tell you that the worst room in the house, the one the unfortunate lady is supposed to have occupied, is locked up, you know, the one on the second floor. I imagine Wilkes mentioned it to you.'

'Yes, he did,' I replied. 'Said he kept important papers there.'

'Yes; well, he was forced in self-defence to do so ten years ago, and since then the death rate has been lower, but in those forty years twenty people have taken their lives in the house or in the river, and six children have been drowned accidentally. The last case was Lord Passover's butler in 1924. He was seen to run down to the river and leap in. He was pulled out, but had died of shock.

'The people who took the house two years ago left in a week, and threatened to bring an action against Wilkes, but they were warned they had no legal case. And I strongly advise you, more than that, *implore* you, to follow their example, though I can imagine the financial loss and great inconvenience, for that house is a death-trap.'

'I will,' I replied. 'I forgot to mention one thing; when my little boy was so badly frightened he said something about "a green monkey".'

'He did!' said Sir William sharply. 'Well then, it is

absolutely imperative that you should leave at once. You remember I mentioned the death of certain children. Well, in each case they have been found drowned in the reeds just at the end of that lane, and the people about here have a firm belief that "The Green Thing", or "The Green Death" —it is sometimes referred to as the first and sometimes as the other—is connected with danger to children.'

'Have you ever seen anything yourself?' I asked.

'I go to the infernal place as little as possible,' replied Sir William, 'but when I called on your predecessors I most distinctly saw someone leave the drawing-room as we entered it, otherwise all I have noted is a certain dream which recurs with curious regularity. I find myself standing at the end of the lane and watching the river—always in a sort of brassy half-light. And presently something comes floating down the stream. I can see it jerking up and down, and I always feel passionately anxious to see what it may be. At first I think that it is a log, but when it gets exactly opposite me it changes its course and comes towards me, and then I see that it is a dead body, very decomposed. And when it reaches the bank it begins to climb up towards me, and then I am thankful to say I always awake. Sometimes I have thought that one day I shall not wake just then, and that on this occasion something will happen to me, but that is probably merely the silly fancy of an old gentleman who has concerned himself with these singular events rather more than is good for his nerves.'

'That is obviously the explanation,' I said, 'and I am extremely grateful to you. We will leave tomorrow. But don't you think we should attempt to devise some means by which other people may be spared this sort of thing, and this brute Wilkes be prevented from letting the house again?'

'I certainly do so, and we will discuss it further on some other occasion. And now go and pack!'

A very great and charming gentleman, Sir William, I reflected, as I walked back to the Red Lodge.

Tim seemed to have recovered excellently well, but I thought it wise to keep him out of the house as much as possible, so while Mary and the maids packed after lunch I went with him for a walk through the fields. We took our time, and it was only when the sky grew black and there was a distant rumble of thunder and a menacing little breeze came from the west that we turned to come back. We had to hurry, and as we reached the meadow next to the house there came a ripping flash and the storm broke. We started to run for the door into the garden when I tripped over my bootlace, which had come undone, and fell. Tim ran on. I had just tied the lace and was on my feet again when I saw something slip through the door. It was green, thin, tall. It seemed to glance back at me, and what should have been its face was a patch of soused slime. At that moment Tim saw it, screamed, and ran for the river. The figure turned and followed him, and before I could reach him hovered over him. Tim screamed again and flung himself in. A moment later I passed through a green and stenching film and dived after him. I found him writhing in the reeds and brought him to the bank. I ran with him in my arms to the house, and I shall not forget Mary's face as she saw us from the bedroom window.

By nine o'clock we were all in an hotel in London, and the Red Lodge an evil, fading memory. I shut the front door when I had packed them all into the car. As I took hold of the knob I felt a quick and powerful pressure from the other side, and it shut with a crash. The Permanent Occupants of the Red Lodge were in sole possession once more.

The Furnished Room

O. HENRY

It is not just in college buildings and country houses that ghosts are to be found: experience shows that they are just as likely to appear in the heart of a big city in a flat or tenement block. Such everyday locations do not very often occur in ghost stories, but when they do—as in this next story by O. Henry—they have an especially unusual and bizarre quality. O. Henry, whose real name was William Sidney Porter, is recognised as one of this century's great masters of the short story, and is among the most revered of modern American writers. After he had spent the early part of his life in a variety of jobs—not to mention a term in prison—he took to writing about the life and times of the ordinary people of American cities. Despite the immediate acclaim which greeted his stories, O. Henry continued to live and work among those he wrote about, and drifted from one place to another, one experience to the next. 'I am a man who has made a lifetime search after what is to be found beyond death,' he once said, adding that he was 'haunted by the shades of people who lived in rooms before me and walked the streets ahead of me.' One particular evening he provided dinner for two penniless girls, the older of whom told him the sad story of her love affair. Unbeknownst to her, she said, after they had quarrelled and parted, her lover had tried to trace her by visiting the apartments in which she had stayed—until, in despair at ever finding her, he had committed suicide in one of the meanest rooms. O. Henry was entranced by the story, said his biographer and friend, Professor Alphonso Smith. 'He scarcely noticed when the girls left. He had tracked an idea. It possessed him. He already smelled the fragrance of mignonette.' Whirling through his mind was the remembrance of a 'presence' he had once felt in an apartment in which he had stayed—and from the combination of his own experience and the girl's story came "The Furnished Room".

Restless, shifting, fugacious as time itself is a certain vast bulk of the population of the red brick district of the lower West Side. Homeless, they have a hundred homes. They flit from furnished room to furnished room, transients forever —transients in abode, transients in heart and mind. They sing "Home, Sweet Home" in ragtime; they carry their *lares et penates* in a bandbox; their vine is entwined about a picture hat; a rubber plant is their fig tree.

Hence the houses of this district, having had a thousand dwellers, should have a thousand tales to tell, mostly dull ones, no doubt, but it would be strange if there could not be found a ghost or two in the wake of all these vagrant guests.

One evening after dark a young man prowled among these crumbling red mansions, ringing their bells. At the twelfth he rested his lean hand-luggage upon the step and wiped the dust from his hat-band and forehead. The bell sounded faint and far away in some remote, hollow depths.

To the door of this, the twelfth house whose bell he had

rung, came a housekeeper who made him think of an unwholesome, surfeited worm that had eaten its nut to a hollow shell and now sought to fill the vacancy with edible lodgers.

He asked if there was a room to let.

'Come in,' said the housekeeper. Her voice came from her throat; her throat seemed lined with fur. 'I have the third floor back, vacant since a week back. Should you wish to look at it?'

The young man followed her up the stairs. A faint light from no particular source mitigated the shadows of the halls. They trod noiselessly upon a stair carpet that its own loom would have forsworn. It seemed to have become vegetable; to have degenerated in that rank, sunless air to lush lichen or spreading moss that grew in patches to the staircase and was viscid under the foot like organic matter. At each turn of the stairs were vacant niches in the wall. Perhaps plants had once been set within them. If so they had died in that foul and tainted air. It may be that statues of the saints had stood there, but it was not difficult to conceive that imps and devils had dragged them forth in the darkness and down to the unholy depths of some furnished pit below.

'This is the room,' said the housekeeper, from her furry throat. 'It's a nice room. It ain't often vacant. I had some most elegant people in it last summer—no trouble at all, and paid in advance to the minute. The water's at the end of the hall. Sprowls and Mooney kept it three months. They done a vaudeville sketch. Miss B'retta Sprowls—you may have heard of her—Oh, that was just the stage names—right there over the dresser is where the marriage certificate hung, framed. The gas is here, and you see there is plenty of closet room. It's a room everybody likes. It never stays idle long.'

'Do you have many theatrical people rooming here?' asked the young man.

'They comes and goes. A good proportion of my lodgers is connected with theatres. Yes, sir, this is the theatrical district.

Actor people never stays long anywhere. I get my share. Yes, they comes and they goes.'

He engaged the room, paying for a week in advance. He was tired, he said, and would take possession at once. He counted out the money. The room had been made ready, she said, even to towels and water. As the housekeeper moved away he put, for the thousandth time, the question that he carried at the end of his tongue.

'A young girl—Miss Vashner—Miss Eloise Vashner—do you remember such a one among your lodgers? She would be singing on the stage, most likely. A fair girl, of medium height, and slender, with reddish, gold hair and a dark mole near her left eyebrow.'

'No, I don't remember the name. Them stage people has names they change as often as their rooms. They comes and they goes. No, I don't call that one to mind.'

No. Always no. Five months of ceaseless interrogation and the inevitable negative. So much time spent by day in questioning managers, agents, schools and choruses; by night among the audiences of theatres from all-star casts down to music halls so low that he dreaded to find what he most hoped for. He who had loved her best had tried to find her. He was sure that since her disappearance from home this great, water-girt city held her somewhere, but it was like a monstrous quicksand, shifting its particles constantly, with no foundation, its upper granules of today buried tomorrow in ooze and slime.

The furnished room received its latest guest with a first glow of pseudo-hospitality, a hectic, haggard, perfunctory welcome like the specious smile of a demirep. The sophistical comfort came in reflected gleams from the decayed furniture, the ragged brocade upholstery of a couch and two chairs, a foot-wide cheap pier glass between the two windows, from one or two gilt picture frames and a brass bedstead in a corner.

The guest reclined, inert, upon a chair, while the room,

confused in speech as though it were an apartment in Babel, tried to discourse to him of its divers tenantry.

A polychromatic rug like some brilliant-flowered rectangular, tropical islet lay surrounded by a billowy sea of soiled matting. Upon the gay-papered wall were those pictures that pursue the homeless one from house to house—The Huguenot Lovers, The First Quarrel, The Wedding Breakfast, Psyche at the Fountain, The mantel's chastely severe outline was ingloriously veiled behind some pert drapery drawn rakishly askew like the sashes of the Amazonian ballet. Upon it was some desolate flotsam cast aside by the room's marooned when a lucky sail had borne them to a fresh port—a trifling vase or two, pictures of actresses, a medicine bottle, some stray cards out of a deck.

One by one, as the characters of a cryptograph become explicit, the little signs left by the furnished room's procession of guests developed a significance. The threadbare space in the rug in front of the dresser told that lovely women had marched in the throng. Tiny fingerprints on the wall spoke of little prisoners trying to feel their way to sun and air. A splattered stain, raying like a shadow of a bursting bomb, witnessed where a hurled glass or bottle had splintered with its contents against the wall. Across the pier glass had been scrawled with a diamond in staggering letters the name 'Marie'. It seemed that the succession of dwellers in the furnished room had turned in fury—perhaps tempted beyond forbearance by its garish coldness—and wreaked upon it their passions. The furniture was chipped and bruised, the couch, distorted by bursting springs, seemed a horrible monster that had been slain during the stress of some grotesque convulsion. Some more potent upheaval had cloven a great slice from the marble mantel. Each plank in the floor owned its particular cant and shriek as from a separate and individual agony. It seemed incredible that all this malice and injury had been wrought upon the room by those who had called it for a time their home; and yet it may have been the cheated home instinct surviving blindly, the resentful rage at false household gods that had kindled their wrath. A hut that is our own we can sweep and adorn and cherish.

The young tenant in the chair allowed these thoughts to file, soft-shod, through his mind, while there drifted into the room furnished sounds and furnished scents. He heard in one room a tittering and incontinent, slack laughter; in others the monologue of a scold, the rattling of dice, a lullaby, and one crying dully; above him a banjo tinkled with spirit. Doors banged somewhere, the elevated trains roared intermittently; a cat yowled miserably upon a back fence. And he breathed the breath of the house—a dank savour rather than a smell—a cold, musty effluvium as from underground vaults mingled with the reeking exhalations of linoleum and mildewed and rotten woodwork.

Then, suddenly, as he rested there, the room was filled with the strong, sweet odour of mignonette. It came as upon a single buffet of wind with such sureness and fragrance and emphasis that it almost seemed a living visitant. And the man cried aloud: 'What, dear?' as if he had been called, and sprang up and faced about. The rich odour clung to him and wrapped him around. He reached out his arms for it, all his senses for the time confused and commingled. How could one be peremptorily called by an odour? Surely it must have been a sound. But, was it not the sound that had touched, that had caressed him?

'She has been in this room,' he cried, and he sprang to wrest from it a token, for he knew he would recognise the smallest thing that had belonged to her or that she had touched. This enveloping scent of mignonette, the odour that she had loved and made her own—whence came it?

The room had been but carelessly set in order. Scattered upon the flimsy dresser scarf were half a dozen hairpins—those discreet, indistinguishable friends of womankind, feminine of gender, infinite of mood and uncommunicative of tense. These he ignored, conscious of their triumphant lack of identity. Ransacking the drawers of the dresser he came upon a discarded, tiny, ragged handkerchief. He pressed it to his face. It was racy and insolent with heliotrope; he hurled it to the floor. In another drawer he found odd buttons, a theatre programme, a pawnbroker's card, two lost marshmallows, a book on the divination of dreams. In the last was a woman's black satin hair-bow, which halted him, poised between ice and fire. But the black satin hairbow also is femininity's demure, impersonal, common ornament, and tells no tales.

And then he traversed the room like a hound on the scent, skimming the walls, considering the corners of the bulging matting on his hands and knees, rummaging mantel and tables, the curtains and hangings, the drunken cabinet in the corner, for a visible sign, unable to perceive that she was there beside, around, against, within, above him, clinging to him, wooing him, calling him so poignantly through the finer senses that even his grosser ones became cognisant of the call. Once again he answered loudly: 'Yes, dear!' and turned wild-eyed, to gaze on vacancy, for he could not yet discern form and colour and love and outstretched arms in the odour of mignonette. Oh, God! whence that odour, and since when have odours had a voice to call? Thus he groped.

He burrowed in crevices and corners, and found corks and cigarettes. These he passed in passive contempt. But once he found in a fold of the matting a half-smoked cigar, and this he ground beneath his heel with a green and trenchant oath. He sifted the room from end to end. He found dreary and ignoble small records of many a peripatetic tenant; but of her whom he sought, and who may have lodged there, and whose spirit seemed to hover there, he found no trace.

And then he thought of the housekeeper.

He ran from the haunted room downstairs and to a door that showed a crack of light. She came out to his knock. He smothered his excitement as best he could.

'Will you tell me, madam,' he besought her, 'who occupied the room I have before I came?'

'Yes, sir. I can tell you again. 'Twas Sprowls and Mooney, as I said. Miss B'retta Sprowls it was in the theatres, but Missis Mooney she was. My house is well known for respectability. The marriage certificate hung, framed, on a nail over——'

'What kind of a lady was Miss Sprowls—in looks, I mean?'

'Why, black-haired, sir, short, and stout, with a comical face. They left a week ago Tuesday.'

'And before they occupied it?'

'Why, there was a single gentleman connected with the draying business. He left owing me a week. Before him was Missis Crowder and her two children, they stayed four months; and back of them was old Mr. Doyle, whose sons paid for him. He kept the room six months. That goes back a year, sir, and further I do not remember.'

He thanked her and crept back to his room. The room was dead. The essence that had vivified it was gone. The perfume of mignonette had departed. In its place was the old, stale odour of mouldy house furniture, of atmosphere in storage.

The ebbing of his hope drained his faith. He sat staring at the yellow, singing gaslight. Soon he walked to the bed and began to tear the sheets into strips. With the blade of his knife he drove them tightly into every crevice around windows and door. When all was snug and taut he turned out the light, turned the gas full on again and laid himself gratefully upon the bed.

It was Mrs McCool's night to go with the can for beer. So she fetched it and sat with Mrs Purdy in one of those subterranean retreats where house-keepers forgather and the worm dieth seldom.

'I rented out my third floor, back, this evening,' said Mrs

Purdy, across a fine circle of foam. 'A young man took it. He went up to bed two hours ago.'

'Now, did ye, Missis Purdy, ma'am?' said Mrs McCool, with intense admiration. 'You do be a wonder for rentin' rooms of that kind. And did ye tell him, then?' she concluded in a husky whisper, laden with misery.

'Rooms,' said Mrs Purdy, in her furriest tones, 'are furnished for to rent. I did not tell him, Mrs McCool.'

' 'Tis right ye are, ma'am, 'tis by renting rooms we kape alive. Ye have the rale sense for business, ma'am. There be many people will rayjict the rentin' of a room if they be tould a suicide has been after dyin' in the bed of it.'

'As you say, we has our living to be making,' remarked Mrs Purdy.

'Yis, ma'am, 'tis true. 'Tis just one wake ago this day I helped ye lay out the third floor, back. A pretty slip of a colleen she was to be killin' herself wid the gas—a swate little face she had, Mrs Purdy, ma'am.'

'She'd a-been called handsome, as you say,' said Mrs Purdy, assenting but critical, 'but for that mole she had a-growin' by her left eyebrow. Do fill up your glass again, Missis McCool.'

A Haunted Island

ALGERNON BLACKWOOD

Ghosts are not confined to any particular areas of the world, of course, and indeed every continent and virtually all nations have their own special tales of spirits and phantoms. So, in the next few selections I have assembled some fairly representative stories of different kinds of ghosts from far flung parts of the globe. By no means exhaustive, they will at least indicate to the reader the richness of supernatural lore wherever one goes. Perhaps no other modern writer has a more widespread experience of ghostly phenomena than Algernon Blackwood whose travels have taken him across Europe, over the American continent and even into the East. Although a writer of short stories since his youth—when his adventures ranged from gold mining in Canada to running an hotel in New York—Blackwood earned his fame as a broadcaster, reading his chilling tales to late night audiences in the 1940's. Several of his short stories are based on personal encounters with the supernatural, including the 'strange, slithering noises' in a New York flat which he turned into "A Suspicious Gift" and the 'cowled figures' which became the basis of the French black magic story "Ancient Sorceries". On his own admission, the strangest of all these encounters took place on a remote Canadian island where he camped for a while with some other young friends. They were forced to leave him alone for one night, and during those hours he underwent 'an experience with the paranormal which nearly turned my reason'. To hint at what happened would spoil the suspense of "A Haunted Island" ...

The following events occurred on a small island of isolated position in a large Canadian lake, to whose cool waters the inhabitants of Montreal and Toronto flee for rest and recreation in the hot months. It is only to be regretted that events of such peculiar interest to the genuine student of the psychical should be entirely uncorroborated. Such unfortunately, however, is the case.

Our own party of nearly twenty had returned to Montreal that very day, and I was left in solitary possession for a week or two longer, in order to accomplish some important 'reading' for the law which I had foolishly neglected during the summer.

It was late in September, and the big trout and maskinonge were stirring themselves in the depths of the lake and beginning slowly to move up to the surface waters as the north winds and early frosts lowered their temperature. Already the maples were crimson and gold, and the wild laughter of the loons echoed in sheltered bays that never knew their strange cry in the summer.

With a whole island to oneself, a two-storey cottage, a canoe, and only the chipmunks, and the farmer's weekly visit with eggs and bread, to disturb one, the opportunities for hard reading might be very great. It all depends!

The rest of the party had gone off with many warnings to beware of Indians, and not to stay late enough to be the victim of a frost that thinks nothing of forty below zero. After they had gone, the loneliness of the situation made itself unpleasantly felt. There were no other islands within six or seven miles, and though the mainland forests lay a couple of miles behind me, they stretched for a very great distance unbroken by any signs of human habitation. But, though the island was completely deserted and silent, the rocks and trees that had echoed human laughter and voices almost every hour of the day for two months could not fail to retain some memories of it all; and I was not surprised to fancy I heard a shout or a cry as I passed from rock to rock, and more than once to imagine that I heard my own name called aloud.

In the cottage there were six tiny little bedrooms divided from one another by plain unvarnished partitions of pine. A wooden bedstead, a mattress, and a chair, stood in each room, but I only found two mirrors, and one of these was broken.

The boards creaked a good deal as I moved about, and the signs of occupation were so recent that I could hardly believe I was alone. I half expected to find someone left behind, still trying to crowd into a box more than it would hold. The door of one room was stiff, and refused for a moment to open, and it required very little persuasion to imagine someone was holding the handle on the inside, and that when it opened I should meet a pair of human eyes.

A thorough search of the floor led me to select as my own sleeping quarters a little room with a diminutive balcony over the veranda roof. The room was very small, but the bed was large, and had the best mattress of them all. It was situated directly over the sitting-room where I should live and do my 'reading', and the miniature window looked out to the rising sun. With the exception of a narrow path which led from the front door and veranda through the trees to the boat-landing, the island was densely covered with maples, hemlocks, and cedars. The trees gathered in round the cottage so closely that the slightest wind made the branches scrape the roof and tap the wooden walls. A few moments after sunset the darkness became impenetrable, and ten yards beyond the glare of the lamps that shone through the sitting-room windows—of which there were four—you could not see an inch before your nose, nor move a step without running up against a tree.

The rest of that day I spent moving my belongings from my tent to the sitting-room, taking stock of the contents of the larder, and chopping enough wood for the stove to last me for a week. After that, just before sunset, I went round the island a couple of times in my canoe for precaution's sake. I had never dreamed of doing this before, but when a man is alone he does things that never occur to him when he is one of a large party.

How lonely the island seemed when I landed again! The sun was down, and twilight is unknown in these northern regions. The darkness comes up at once. The canoe safely pulled up and turned over on her face, I groped my way up the little narrow pathway to the veranda. The six lamps were soon burning merrily in the front room; but in the kitchen, where I 'dined', the shadows were so gloomy, and the lamplight was so inadequate, that the stars could be seen peeping through the cracks between the rafters.

I turned in early that night. Though it was calm and there was no wind, the creaking of my bedstead and the musical gurgle of the water over the rocks below were not the only sounds that reached my ears. As I lay awake, the appalling emptiness of the house grew upon me. The corridors and vacant rooms seemed to echo innumerable footsteps, shufflings, the rustle of skirts, and a constant undertone of whispering. When sleep at length overtook me, the breathings and noises, however, passed gently to mingle with the voices of my dreams.

A week passed by, and the 'reading' progressed favourably. On the tenth day of my solitude, a strange thing happened. I awoke after a good night's sleep to find myself possessed with a marked repugnance for my room. The air seemed to stifle me. The more I tried to define the cause of this dislike, the more unreasonable it appeared. There was something about the room that made me afraid. Absurd as it seems, this feeling clung to me obstinately while dressing, and more than once I caught myself shivering, and conscious of an inclination to get out of the room as quickly as possible. The more I tried to laugh it away, the more real it became; and when at last I was dressed, and went out into the passage, and downstairs into the kitchen, it was with feelings of relief, such as I might imagine would accompany one's escape from the presence of a dangerous contagious disease.

While cooking my breakfast, I carefully recalled every night spent in the room, in the hope that I might in some way connect the dislike I now felt with some disagreeable incident that had occurred in it. But the only thing I could recall was one stormy night when I suddenly awoke and heard the boards creaking so loudly in the corridor that I was convinced there were people in the house. So certain was I of this, that I had descended the stairs, gun in hand, only to find the doors and windows securely fastened, and the mice and blackbeetles in sole possession of the floor. This was certainly not sufficient to account for the strength of my feelings.

The morning hours I spent in steady reading; and when I broke off in the middle of the day for a swim and luncheon, I was very much surprised, if not a little alarmed, to find that my dislike for the room had, if anything, grown stronger. Going upstairs to get a book, I experienced the most marked aversion to entering the room, and while within I was conscious all the time of an uncomfortable feeling that was half uneasiness and half apprehension. The result of it was that, instead of reading, I spent the afternoon on the water paddling and fishing, and when I got home about sundown, brought with me half a dozen delicious black bass for the supper-table and the larder.

As sleep was an important matter to me at this time, I had decided that if my aversion to the room was so strongly marked on my return as it had been before, I would move my bed down into the sitting-room, and sleep there. This was, I argued, in no sense a concession to an absurd and fanciful fear, but simply a precaution to ensure a good night's sleep. A bad night involved the loss of the next day's reading, —a loss I was not prepared to incur.

I accordingly moved my bed downstairs into a corner of the sitting-room facing the door, and was moreover uncommonly glad when the operation was completed, and the door of the bedroom closed finally upon the shadows, the silence, and the strange *fear* that shared the room with them.

The croaking stroke of the kitchen clock sounded the hour of eight as I finished washing up my few dishes, and closing the kitchen door behind me, passed into the front room. All the lamps were lit, and their reflectors, which I had polished up during the day, threw a blaze of light into the room.

Outside the night was still and warm. Not a breath of air was stirring; the waves were silent, the trees motionless, and heavy clouds hung like an oppressive curtain over the heavens. The darkness seemed to have rolled up with unusual swiftness, and not the faintest glow of colour remained to show where the sun had set. There was present in the atmosphere that ominous and overwhelming silence which so often precedes the most violent storms.

I sat down to my books with my brain unusually clear, and in my heart the pleasant satisfaction of knowing that five black bass were lying in the ice-house, and that tomorrow morning the old farmer would arrive with fresh bread and eggs. I was soon absorbed in my books.

As the night wore on the silence deepened. Even the chipmunks were still; and the boards of the floors and walls cease creaking. I read on steadily till, from the gloomy shadows of the kitchen, came the hoarse sound of the clock striking nine. How loud the strokes sounded! They were like blows of a big hammer. I closed one book and opened another, feeling that I was just warming up to my work.

This, however, did not last long. I presently found that I was reading the same paragraphs over twice, simple paragraphs that did not require such effort. Then I noticed that my mind began to wander to other things, and the effort to recall my thoughts became harder with each digression. Concentration was growing momentarily more difficult. Presently I discovered that I had turned over two pages instead of one, and had not noticed my mistake until I was well down the page. This was becoming serious. What was the disturbing influence? It could not be physical fatigue. On the contrary, my mind was unusually alert, and in a more receptive condition than usual. I made a new and determined effort to read, and for a short time succeeded in giving my whole attention to my subject. But in a very few moments again I found myself leaning back in my chair, staring vacantly into space.

Something was evidently at work in my subconsciousness. There was something I had neglected to do. Perhaps the kitchen door and windows were not fastened. I accordingly went to see, and found that they were! The fire perhaps needed attention. I went in to see, and found that it was all right! I looked at the lamps, went upstairs into every bedroom in turn, and then went round the house, and even into the ice-house. Nothing was wrong; everything was in its place. Yet something *was* wrong! The conviction grew stronger and stronger within me.

When I at length settled down to my books again and tried to read, I became aware, for the first time, that the room seemed growing cold. Yet the day had been oppressively warm, and evening had brought no relief. The six big lamps, moreover, gave out heat enough to warm the room pleasantly. But a chilliness, that perhaps crept up from the lake, made itself felt in the room, and caused me to get up to close the glass door opening on to the veranda.

For a brief moment I stood looking out at the shaft of light that fell from the windows and shone some little distance down the pathway, and out for a few feet into the lake.

As I looked I saw a canoe glide into the pathway of light, and immediately crossing it, pass out of sight again into the darkness. It was perhaps a hundred feet from the shore, and it moved swiftly.

I was surprised that a canoe should pass the island at that time of night, for all the summer visitors from the other side of the lake had gone home weeks before, and the island was a long way out of any line of water traffic.

My reading from this moment did not make very good progress, for somehow the picture of that canoe, gliding so dimly and swiftly across the narrow track of light on the black waters, silhouetted itself against the background of my mind with singular vividness. It kept coming between my eyes and the printed page. The more I thought about it the more surprised I became. It was of larger build than any I had seen during the past summer months, and was more like the old Indian war canoes with the high curving bows and stern and wide beam. The more I tried to read, the less success attended my efforts; and finally I closed my books and went out on the veranda to walk up and down a bit, and shake the chilliness out of my bones.

The night was perfectly still, and as dark as imaginable. I stumbled down the path to the little landing wharf, where the water made the very faintest of gurgling under the timbers. The sound of a big tree falling in the mainland forest, far across the lake, stirred echoes in the heavy air, like the first guns of a distant night attack. No other sound disturbed the stillness that reigned supreme.

As I stood upon the wharf in the broad splash of light that

followed me from the sitting-room windows, I saw another canoe cross the pathway of uncertain light upon the water, and disappear at once into the impenetrable gloom that lay beyond. This time I saw more distinctly than before. It was like the former canoe, a big birch-bark, with high-crested bows and stern and broad beam. It was paddled by two Indians, of whom the one in the stern—the steerer— appeared to be a very large man. I could see this very plainly; and though the second canoe was much nearer the island than the first, I judged that they were both on their way home to the Government Reservation, which was situated some fifteen miles away upon the mainland.

I was wondering in my mind what could possibly bring any Indians down to this part of the lake at such an hour of the night, when a third canoe, of precisely similar build, and also occupied by two Indians, passed silently round the end of the wharf. This time the canoe was very much nearer shore, and it suddenly flashed into my mind that the three canoes were in reality one and the same, and that only one canoe was circling the island!

This was by no means a pleasant reflection, because, if it were the correct solution of the unusual appearance of the three canoes in this lonely part of the lake at so late an hour, the purpose of the two men could only reasonably be con- sidered to be in some way connected with myself. I had never known of the Indians attempting any violence upon the settlers who shared the wild, inhospitable country with them; at the same time, it was not beyond the region of possibility to suppose. . . . But then I did not care even to think of such hideous possibilities, and my imagination immediately sought relief in all manner of other solutions to the problem, which indeed came readily enough to my mind, but did not succeed in recommending themselves to my reason.

Meanwhile, by a sort of instinct, I stepped back out of the bright light in which I had hitherto been standing, and waited in the deep shadow of a rock to see if the canoe would again make its appearance. Here I could see, without being seen, and the precaution seemed a wise one.

After less than five minutes the canoe, as I had anticipated, made its fourth appearance. This time it was not twenty yards from the wharf, and I saw that the Indians meant to land. I recognised the two men as those who had passed before, and the steerer was certainly an immense fellow. It was unquestionably the same canoe. There could be no longer any doubt that for some purpose of their own the men had been going round and round the island for some time, waiting for an opportunity to land. I strained my eyes to follow them in the darkness, but the night had completely swallowed them up, and not even the faintest swish of the paddles reached my ears as the Indians plied their long and powerful strokes. The canoe would be round again in a few moments, and this time it was possible that the men might land. It was well to be prepared. I knew nothing of their intentions, and two to one (when the two are big Indians!) late at night on a lonely island was not exactly my idea of pleasant intercourse.

In a corner of the sitting-room, leaning up against the back wall, stood my Marlin rifle, with ten cartridges in the magazine and one lying snugly in the greased breech. There was just time to get up to the house and take up a position of defence in that corner. Without an instant's hesitation I ran up to the veranda, carefully picking my way among the trees, so as to avoid being seen in the light. Entering the room, I shut the door leading to the veranda, and as quickly as possible turned out every one of the six lamps. To be in a room so brilliantly lighted, where my every movement could be observed from outside, while I could see nothing but impenetrable darkness at every window, was by all laws of warfare an unnecessary concession to the enemy. And this enemy, if enemy it was to be, was far too wily and dangerous to be granted any such advantages.

I stood in the corner of the room with my back against the wall, and my hand on the cold rifle-barrel. The table, covered with my books, lay between me and the door, but for the first few minutes after the lights were out the darkness was so intense that nothing could be discerned at all. Then, very gradually, the outline of the room became visible, and the framework of the windows began to shape itself dimly before my eyes.

After a few minutes the door (its upper half of glass), and the two windows that looked out upon the front veranda, became specially distinct; and I was glad that this was so, because if the Indians came up to the house I should be able to see their approach, and gather something of their plans. Nor was I mistaken, for there presently came to my ears the peculiar hollow sound of a canoe landing and being carefully dragged up over the rocks. The paddles I distinctly heard being placed underneath, and the silence that ensued thereupon I rightly interpreted to mean that the Indians were stealthily approaching the house. . . .

While it would be absurd to claim that I was not alarmed —even frightened—at the gravity of the situation and its possible outcome, I speak the whole truth when I say that I was not overwhelmingly afraid for myself. I was conscious that even at this stage of the night I was passing into a psychical condition in which my sensations seemed no longer normal. Physical fear at no time entered into the nature of my feelings; and though I kept my hand upon my rifle the greater part of the night, I was all the time conscious that its assistance could be of little avail against the terrors that I had to face. More than once I seemed to feel most curiously that I was in no real sense a part of the proceedings, nor actually involved in them, but that I was playing the part of a spectator—a spectator, moreover, on a psychic rather than on a material plane. Many of my sensations that night were too vague for definite description and analysis, but the main feeling that will stay with me to the end of my days is the awful horror of it all, and the miserable sensation that if the strain had lasted a little longer than was actually the case my mind must inevitably have given way.

Meanwhile I stood still in my corner, and waited patiently for what was to come. The house was as still as the grave, but the inarticulate voices of the night sang in my ears, and I seemed to hear the blood running in my veins and dancing in my pulses.

If the Indians came to the back of the house, they would find the kitchen door and window securely fastened. They could not get in there without making considerable noise, which I was bound to hear. The only mode of getting in was by means of the door that faced me, and I kept my eyes glued on that door without taking them off for the smallest fraction of a second.

My sight adapted itself every minute better to the darkness. I saw the table that nearly filled the room, and left only a narrow passage on each side. I could also make out the straight backs of the wooden chairs pressed up against it, and could even distinguish my papers and inkstand lying on the white oilcloth covering. I thought of the gay faces that had gathered round that table during the summer, and I longed for the sunlight as I had never longed for it before.

Less than three feet to my left the passage-way led to the kitchen, and the stairs leading to the bedrooms above commenced in the passage-way but almost in the sitting-room itself. Through the windows I could see the dim motionless outlines of the trees: not a leaf stirred, not a branch moved.

A few moments of this awful silence, and then I was aware of a soft tread on the boards of the veranda, so stealthy that it seemed an impression directly on my brain rather than upon the nerves of hearing. Immediately afterwards a black figure darkened the glass door, and I perceived that a face was pressed against the upper panes. A shiver ran down my back, and my hair was conscious of a tendency to rise and stand at right angles to my head.

It was the figure of an Indian, broad-shouldered and immense; indeed, the largest figure of a man I have ever seen outside of a circus hall. By some power of light that seemed to generate itself in the brain, I saw the strong dark face with the aquiline nose and high cheek-bones flattened against the glass. The direction of the gaze I could not determine; but faint gleams of light as the big eyes rolled round and showed their whites, told me plainly that no corner of the room escaped their searching.

For what seemed fully five minutes the dark figure stood there, with the huge shoulders bent forward so as to bring the head down to the level of the glass; while behind him, though not nearly so large, the shadowy form of the other Indian swayed to and fro like a bent tree. While I waited in an agony of suspense and agitation for their next movement little currents of icy sensation ran up and down my spine and my heart seemed alternately to stop beating and then start off again with terrifying rapidity. They must have heard its thumping and the singing of the blood in my head! Moreover, I was conscious, as I felt a cold stream of perspiration trickle down my face, of a desire to scream, to shout, to bang the walls like a child, to make a noise, or do anything that would relieve the suspense and bring things to a speedy climax.

It was probably this inclination that led me to another discovery, for when I tried to bring my rifle from behind my back to raise it and have it pointed at the door ready to fire, I found that I was powerless to move. The muscles, paralysed by this strange fear, refused to obey the will. Here indeed was a terrifying complication!

There was a faint sound of rattling at the brass knob, and the door was pushed open a couple of inches. A pause of a few seconds, and it was pushed open still further. Without a

sound of footsteps that was appreciable to my ears, the two
figures glided into the room, and the man behind gently
closed the door after him.

They were alone with me between the four walls. Could
they see me standing there, so still and straight in my corner?
Had they, perhaps, already seen me? My blood surged and
sang like the roll of drums in an orchestra; and though I did
my best to suppress my breathing, it sounded like the rushing
of wind through a pneumatic tube.

My suspense as to the next move was soon at an end—
only, however, to give place to a new and keener alarm.
The men had hitherto exchanged no words and no signs, but
there were general indications of a movement across the
room, and whichever way they went they would have to
pass round the table. If they came my way they would have
to pass within six inches of my person. While I was considering this very disagreeable possibility, I perceived that
the smaller Indian (smaller by comparison) suddenly raised
his arm and pointed to the ceiling. The other fellow raised
his head and followed the direction of his companion's arm.
I began to understand at last. They were going upstairs, and
the room directly overhead to which they pointed had been
until this night my bedroom. It was the room in which I had
experienced that very morning so strange a sensation of fear,
and but for which I should then have been lying asleep in
the narrow bed against the window.

The Indians then began to move silently around the room;
they were going upstairs, and they were coming round my
side of the table. So stealthy were their movements that, but
for the abnormally sensitive state of the nerves, I should
never have heard them. As it was, their cat-like tread was
distinctly audible. Like two monstrous black cats they came
round the table towards me, and for the first time I perceived that the smaller of the two dragged something along
the floor behind him. As it trailed along over the floor with
a soft, sweeping sound, I somehow got the impression that it

was a large dead thing with outstretched wings, or a large, spreading cedar branch. Whatever it was, I was unable to see it even in outline, and I was too terrified, even had I possessed the power over my muscles, to move my neck forward in the effort to determine its nature.

Nearer and nearer they came. The leader rested a giant hand upon the table as he moved. My lips were glued together, and the air seemed to burn in my nostrils. I tried to close my eyes, so that I might not see as they passed me ; but my eyelids had stiffened, and refused to obey. Would they never get by me? Sensation seemed also to have left my legs, and it was as if I were standing on mere supports of wood or stone. Worse still, I was conscious that I was losing the power of balance, the power to stand upright, or even to lean backwards against the wall. Some force was drawing me forward, and a dizzy terror seized me that I should lose my balance, and topple forward against the Indians just as they were in the act of passing me.

Even moments drawn out into hours must come to an end some time, and almost before I knew it the figures had passed me and had their feet upon the lower step of the stairs leading to the upper bedrooms. There could not have been six inches between us, and yet I was conscious only of a current of cold air that followed them. They had not touched me, and I was convinced that they had not seen me. Even the trailing thing on the floor behind them had not touched my feet, as I had dreaded it would, and on such an occasion as this I was grateful even for the smallest mercies.

The absence of the Indians from my immediate neighbourhood brought little sense of relief. I stood shivering and shuddering in my corner, and, beyond being able to breathe more freely, I felt no whit less uncomfortable. Also, I was aware that a certain light, which, without apparent source or rays, had enabled me to follow their every gesture and movement, had gone out of the room with their departure. An unnatural darkness now filled the room, and pervaded its every corner so that I could barely make out the positions of the windows and the glass doors.

As I said before, my condition was evidently an abnormal one. The capacity for feeling surprise seemed, as in dreams, to be wholly absent. My senses recorded with unusual accuracy every smallest occurrence, but I was able to draw only the simplest deductions.

The Indians soon reached the top of the stairs, and there they halted for a moment. I had not the faintest clue as to their next movement. They appeared to hesitate. They were listening attentively. Then I heard one of them, who by the weight of his soft tread must have been the giant, cross the narrow corridor and enter the room directly overhead—my own little bedroom. But for the insistence of that unaccountable dread I had experienced there in the morning, I should at that very moment have been lying in the bed with the big Indian in the room standing beside me.

For a space of a hundred seconds there was silence, such as might have existed before the birth of sound. It was followed by a long quivering shriek of terror, which rang out into the night, and ended in a short gulp before it had run its full course. At the same moment the other Indian left his place at the head of the stairs, and joined his companion in the bedroom. I heard the 'thing' trailing behind him along the floor. A thud followed, as of something heavy falling, and then all became as still and silent as before.

It was at this point that the atmosphere, surcharged all day with the electricity of a fierce storm, found relief in a dancing flash of brilliant lightning simultaneously with a crash of loudest thunder. For five seconds every article in the room was visible to me with amazing distinctness, and through the windows I saw the tree trunks standing in solemn rows. The thunder pealed and echoed across the lake and among the distant islands, and the flood-gates of heaven then opened and let out their rain in streaming torrents.

The drops fell with a swift rushing sound upon the still waters of the lake, which leaped up to meet them, and pattered with the rattle of shot on the leaves of the maples and the roof of the cottage. A moment later, and another flash, even more brilliant and of longer duration than the first, lit up the sky from zenith to horizon, and bathed the room momentarily in dazzling whiteness. I could see the rain glistening on the leaves and branches outside. The wind rose suddenly, and in less than a minute the storm that had been gathering all day burst forth in its full fury.

Above all the noisy voices of the elements, the slightest sounds in the room overhead made themselves heard, and in the few seconds of deep silence that followed the shriek of terror and pain I was aware that the movements had commenced again. The men were leaving the room and approaching the top of the stairs. A short pause, and they began to descend. Behind them, tumbling from step to step, I could hear that trailing 'thing' being dragged along. It had become ponderous!

I awaited their approach with a degree of calmness, almost of apathy, which was only explicable on the ground that after a certain point Nature applies her own anæsthetic, and a merciful condition of numbness supervenes. On they came, step by step, nearer and nearer, with the shuffling sound of the burden behind growing louder as they approached.

They were already half-way down the stairs when I was galvanised afresh into a condition of terror by the consideration of a new and horrible possibility. It was the reflection that if another vivid flash of lightning were to come when the shadowy procession was in the room, perhaps when it was actually passing in front of me, I should see everything in detail, and worse, be seen myself! I could only hold my breath and wait—wait while the minutes lengthened into hours, and the procession made its slow progress round the room.

The Indians had reached the foot of the staircase. The form of the huge leader loomed in the doorway of the passage, and the burden with an ominous thud had dropped from the last step to the floor. There was a moment's pause while I saw the Indian turn and stoop to assist his companion. Then the procession moved forward again, entered the room close on my left, and began to move slowly round my side of the table. The leader was already beyond me, and his companion, dragging on the floor behind him the burden, whose confused outline I could dimly make out, was exactly in front of me, when the cavalcade came to a dead halt. At the same moment, with the strange suddenness of thunderstorms, the splash of the rain ceased altogether, and the wind died away into utter silence.

For the space of five seconds my heart seemed to stop beating, and then the worst came. A double flash of lightning lit up the room and its contents with merciless vividness.

The huge Indian leader stood a few feet past me on my right. One leg was stretched forward in the act of taking a step. His immense shoulders were turned towards his companion, and in all their magnificent fierceness I saw the outline of his features. His gaze was directed upon the burden his companion was dragging along the floor; but his profile, with the big aquiline nose, high cheekbone, straight black hair and bold chin, burnt itself in that brief instant into my brain, never again to fade.

Dwarfish, compared with this gigantic figure, appeared the proportions of the other Indian, who, within twelve inches of my face, was stooping over the thing he was dragging in a position that lent to his person the additional horror of deformity. And the burden, lying upon a sweeping cedar branch which he held and dragged by a long stem, was the body of a white man. The scalp had been neatly lifted, and blood lay in a broad smear upon the cheeks and forehead.

Then, for the first time that night, the terror that had

paralysed my muscles and my will lifted its unholy spell from my soul. With a loud cry I stretched out my arms to seize the big Indian by the throat, and, grasping only air, tumbled forward unconscious upon the ground.

I had recognised the body, and *the face was my own!* . . .

It was bright daylight when a man's voice recalled me to consciousness. I was lying where I had fallen, and the farmer was standing in the room with the loaves of bread in his hands. The horror of the night was still in my heart, and as the bluff settler helped me to my feet and picked up the rifle which had fallen with me, with many questions and expressions of condolence, I imagine my brief replies were neither self-explanatory nor even intelligible.

That day, after a thorough and fruitless search of the house, I left the island, and went over to spend my last ten days with the farmer; and when the time came for me to leave, the necessary reading had been accomplished, and my nerves had completely recovered their balance.

On the day of my departure the farmer started early in his big boat with my belongings to row to the point, twelve miles distant, where a little steamer ran twice a week for the accommodation of hunters. Late in the afternoon I went off in another direction in my canoe, wishing to see the island once again, where I had been the victim of so strange an experience.

In due course I arrived there, and made a tour of the island. I also made a search of the little house, and it was not without a curious sensation in my heart that I entered the little upstairs bedroom. There seemed nothing unusual.

Just after I re-embarked, I saw a canoe gliding ahead of me around the curve of the island. A canoe was an unusual sight at this time of the year, and this one seemed to have sprung from nowhere. Altering my course a little, I watched it disappear around the next projecting point of rock. It had high curving bows, and there were two Indians in it. I lingered with some excitement, to see if it would appear again round the other side of the island; and in less than five minutes it came into view. There were less than two hundred yards between us, and the Indians, sitting on their haunches, were paddling swiftly in my direction.

I never paddled faster in my life than I did in those next few minutes. When I turned to look again, the Indians had altered their course, and were again circling the island.

The sun was sinking behind the forests on the mainland, and the crimson-coloured clouds of sunset were reflected in the waters of the lake, when I looked round for the last time, and saw the big bark canoe and its two dusky occupants still going round the island. Then the shadows deepened rapidly; the lake grew black, and the night wind blew its first breath in my face as I turned a corner, and a projecting bluff of rock hid from my view both island and canoe.

My Own True Ghost Story

RUDYARD KIPLING

Rudyard Kipling's knowledge of India is familiar to most readers, and his works such as the "Jungle Books" and the "Just So Stories" still enjoy great popularity among all age groups. During his lengthy stay in the continent where he worked as a journalist, Kipling became deeply interested in the local folk lore and apart from learning a great deal about the supernatural traditions had a few encounters with the unknown himself. His famous ghost stories such as "The Phantom Rickshaw" and "The Strange Ride of Morrowbie Jukes" contain elements of personal experience and are tales of style and atmosphere. After his return to England at the turn of the century, his fascination with the ghostly continued unabated, and he came to believe that a wood close to his Sussex home was haunted. 'It is full of a sense of ancient ferocity and evil . . . there is a spirit of some kind there,' he told 'ghost hunter' Robert Thurston Hopkins. 'A very impolite fellow he is, too, for one evening something suddenly gripped me and despite my attempts to walk forward I was gradually forced back. I felt some unseen, unknown power just pushing against me and in the end I was compelled to turn around and leave the wood in a most undignified manner.' It was this landscape of Sussex which inspired him to write the story of "Puck of Pook's Hill". It was here, too, that Kipling's child died, and in memory he wrote the supernatural novella "They", which deals with the ghosts of a group of children and has been described as a 'hymn of love'. Perhaps, though, the most interesting and appropriate story for this particular collection is Kipling's "My Own True Ghost Story" which in its denouement introduces an element of the supernatural which we have not so far encountered.

> As I came through the Desert thus it was—
> As I came through the Desert.
>
> *James Thomson*

This story deals entirely with ghosts. There are, in India, ghosts who take the form of fat, cold, pobby corpses, and hide in trees near the roadside till a traveller passes. Then they drop upon his neck and remain. There are also terrible ghosts of women who have died in childbed. These wander along the pathways at dusk, or hide in the crops near a village, and call seductively. But to answer their call is death in this world and the next. Their feet are turned backwards that all sober men may recognise them. There are ghosts of little children who have been thrown into wells. These haunt wellcurbs and the fringes of jungles, and wail under the stars, or catch women by the wrist and beg to be taken up and carried. These and the corpse-ghosts, however, are only vernacular articles and do not attack Sahibs. No native ghost has yet been authentically reported to have frightened an Englishman; but many English ghosts have scared the life out of both white and black.

Nearly every other station owns a ghost. There are said to be two at Simla, not counting the woman who blows the bellows at Syree *dâk*-bungalow on the Old Road; Mussoorie has a house haunted by a very lively Thing; a White Lady is supposed to do night-watchman round a house in Lahore; Dalhousie says that one of her houses 'repeats' on autumn evenings all the incidents of a horrible horse-and-precipice accident; Murree has a merry ghost, and, now that she has been swept by cholera, will have room for a sorrowful one; there are Officers' Quarters in Mian Mir whose doors open without reason, and whose furniture is guaranteed to creak, not with the heat of June, but with the weight of Invisibles who come to lounge in the chairs; Peshawur possesses houses that none will willingly rent; and there is something—not fever—wrong with a big bungalow in Allahabad. The older Provinces simply bristle with haunted houses, and march phantom armies along their main thoroughfares.

Some of the *dâk*-bungalows on the Grand Trunk Road have handy little cemeteries in their compound—witnesses to the 'changes and chances of this mortal life' in the days when men drove from Calcutta to the North-West. These bungalows are objectionable places to put up in. They are generally very old, always dirty, while the *khansamah* is as ancient as the bungalow. He either chatters senilely, or falls into the long trances of age. In both moods he is useless. If you get angry with him, he refers to some Sahib dead and buried these thirty years, and says that when he was in that Sahib's service not a *khansamah* in the Province could touch him. Then he jabbers and mows and trembles and fidgets among the dishes, and you repent of your irritation.

Not long ago it was my business to live in *dâk*-bungalows. I never inhabited the same house for three nights running, and grew to be learned in the breed. I lived in Government-built ones with red brick walls and rail ceilings, an inventory of the furniture posted in every room, and an excited cobra on the threshold to give welcome. I lived in 'converted' ones—old houses officiating as *dâk*-bungalows—where nothing was in its proper place and there was not even a fowl for dinner. I lived in second-hand palaces where the wind blew through open-work marble tracery just as uncomfortably as through a broken pane. I lived in *dâk*-bungalows where the last entry in the visitors' book was fifteen months old, and where they slashed off the curry-kid's head with a sword. It was my good luck to meet all sorts of men, from sober travelling missionaries and deserters flying from British regiments, to drunken loafers who threw whisky bottles at all who passed; and my still greater good-fortune just to escape a maternity case. Seeing that a fair proportion of the tragedy of our lives in India acted itself in *dâk*-bungalows, I wondered that it had met no ghosts. A ghost that would voluntarily hang about a *dâk*-bungalow would be mad, of course; but so many men have died mad in *dâk*-bungalows that there must be a fair percentage of lunatic ghosts.

In due time I found my ghost, or ghosts rather, for there were two of them.

We will call the bungalow Katmal *dâk*-bungalow; but *that* was the smallest part of the horror. A man with a sensitive hide has no right to sleep in *dâk*-bungalows. He should marry. Katmal *dâk*-bungalow was old and rotten and unrepaired. The floor was of worn brick, the walls were filthy, and the windows were nearly black with grime. It stood on a bypath largely used by native Sub-Deputy Assistants of all kinds, from Finance to Forests; but real Sahibs were rare. The *khansamah*, who was bent nearly double with old age, said so.

When I arrived, there was a fitful, undecided rain on the face of the land, accompanied by a restless wind, and every gust made a noise like the rattling of dry bones in the stiff toddy-palms outside. The *khansamah* completely lost his head on my arrival. He had served a Sahib once. Did I know that Sahib? He gave me the name of a well-known man who has been buried for more than a quarter of a century, and showed me an ancient daguerreotype of that man in his prehistoric youth. I had seen a steel engraving of him at the head of a double volume of Memoirs a month before, and I felt ancient beyond telling.

The day shut in and the *khansamah* went to get me food. He did not go through the pretence of calling it '*khana*',— man's victuals. He said '*ratub*', and that means, among other things, 'grub'—dog's rations. There was no insult in his choice of the term. He had forgotten the other word, I suppose.

While he was cutting up the dead bodies of animals, I settled myself down, after exploring the *dâk*-bungalow. There were three rooms besides my own, which was a corner kennel, each giving into the other through dingy white doors fastened with long iron bars. The bungalow was a very solid one, but the partition-walls of the rooms were almost jerry-built in their flimsiness. Every step or bang of a trunk echoed from my room down the other three, and every footfall came back tremulously from the far walls. For this reason I shut the door. There were no lamps—only candles in long glass shades. An oil wick was set in the bathroom.

For bleak, unadulterated misery that *dâk*-bungalow was the worst of the many that I had ever set foot in. There was no fireplace, and the windows would not open; so a brazier of charcoal would have been useless. The rain and the wind splashed and gurgled and moaned round the house, and the toddy-palms rattled and roared. Half-a-dozen jackals went through the compound singing, and a hyena stood afar off and mocked them. A hyena would convince a Sadducee of the Resurrection of the Dead—the worst sort of Dead. Then came the *ratub*—a curious meal, half native and half English in composition—with the old *khansamah* babbling behind my chair about dead-and-gone English people, and the wind-blown candles playing shadow-bo-peep with the bed and the mosquito-curtains. It was just the sort of dinner and evening to make a man think of every single one of his past sins, and of all the others that he intended to commit if he lived.

Sleep, for several hundred reasons, was not easy. The lamp in the bathroom threw the most absurd shadows into the room, and the wind was beginning to talk nonsense.

Just when the reasons were drowsy with blood-sucking I heard the regular—'Let-us-take-and-heave-him-over' grunt of doolie-bearers in the compound. First one doolie came in, then a second, and then a third. I heard the doolies dumped on the ground, and the shutter in front of my door shook.

'That's some one trying to come in,' I said. But no one spoke, and I persuaded myself that it was the gusty wind. The shutter of the room next to mine was attacked, flung back, and the inner door opened. 'That's some Sub-Deputy Assistant,' I said, 'and he has brought his friends with him. Now they'll talk and spit and smoke for an hour.'

But there were no voices and no footsteps. No one was putting his luggage into the next room. The door shut, and I thanked Providence that I was to be left in peace. But I was curious to know where the doolies had gone. I got out of bed and looked into the darkness. There was never a sign of a doolie. Just as I was getting into bed again, I heard, in the next room, the sound that no man in his senses can possibly mistake—the whir of a billiard-ball down the length of the slate when the striker is stringing for break. No other sound is like it. A minute afterwards there was another whir, and I got into bed. I was not frightened—indeed I was not. I was very curious to know what had become of the doolies. I jumped into bed for that reason.

Next minute I heard the double click of a cannon, and my hair sat up. It is a mistake to say that hair stands up. The skin of the head tightens, and you can feel a faint, prickly bristling all over the scalp. That is one's hair sitting up.

There was a whir and a click, and both sounds could only have been made by one thing—a billiard-ball. I argued the matter out at great length with myself; and the more I argued the less probable it seemed that one bed, one table, and two chairs—all the furniture of the room next to mine—could so exactly duplicate the sounds of a game of billiards. After another cannon, a three-cushion one to judge by the whir, I argued no more. I had found my ghost, and would have given worlds to have escaped from the *dâk*-bungalow. I listened, and with each listen the game grew clearer. There was whir on whir and click on click. Sometimes there was a double click and a whir and another click. Beyond any sort of doubt, people were playing billiards in the next room. And the next room was not big enough to hold a billiard-table!

Between the pauses of the wind I heard the game go forward—stroke after stroke. I tried to believe that I could not hear voices; but that attempt was a failure.

Do you know what fear is? Not ordinary fear of insult, injury, or death, but abject, quivering dread of something that you cannot see—fear that dries the inside of the mouth and half of the throat—fear that makes you sweat on the palms of the hands, and gulp in order to keep the uvula at work? This is a fine Fear—a great cowardice, and must be felt to be appreciated. The very improbability of billiards in a *dâk*-bungalow proved the reality of the thing. No man—drunk or sober—could imagine a game at billiards, or invent the spitting crack of a 'screw-cannon'.

A severe course of *dâk*-bungalows has this disadvantage—it breeds infinite credulity. If a man said to a confirmed *dâk*-bungalow-haunter: 'There is a corpse in the next room, and there's a mad girl in the next one, and the woman and man on that camel have just eloped from a place sixty miles away,' the hearer would not disbelieve, because he would know that nothing is too wild, grotesque, or horrible to happen in a *dâk*-bungalow.

This credulity, unfortunately, extends to ghosts. A rational person fresh from his own house would have turned on his side and slept. I did not. So surely as I was given up for a dry carcass by the scores of things in the bed, because the bulk of

my blood was in my heart, so surely did I hear every stroke
of a long game at billiards played in the echoing room behind
the iron-barred door. My dominant fear was that the players
might want a marker. It was an absurd fear; because
creatures who could play in the dark would be above such
superfluities. I only know that that was my terror, and it was
real.

After a long, long while the game stopped, and the door
banged. I slept because I was dead tired. Otherwise I should
have preferred to have kept awake. Not for everything in
Asia would I have dropped the door-bar and peered into the
dark of the next room.

When the morning came I considered that I had done well
and wisely, and inquired for the means of departure.

'By the way, *khansamah*,' I said, 'what were those three
doolies doing in my compound in the night?'

'There were no doolies,' said the *khansamah*.

I went into the next room, and the daylight streamed
through the open door. I was immensely brave. I would, at
that hour, have played Black Pool with the owner of the big
Black Pool down below.

'Has this place always been a *dâk*-bungalow?' I asked.

'No,' said the *khansamah*. 'Ten or twenty years ago, I have
forgotten how long, it was a billiard-room.'

'A what?'

'A billiard-room for the Sahibs who built the Railway. I
was *khansamah* then in the big house where all the Railway-
Sahibs lived, and I used to come across with brandy-*shrab*.
These three rooms were all one, and they held a big table on
which the Sahibs played every evening. But the Sahibs are
all dead now, and the Railway runs, you say, nearly to
Kabul.'

'Do you remember anything about the Sahibs?'

'It is long ago, but I remember that one Sahib, a fat man,
and always angry, was playing here one night, and he said to
me: "Mangal Khan, brandy-*pani do*," and I filled the glass,

and he bent over the table to strike, and his head fell lower and lower till it hit the table, and his spectacles came off, and when we—the Sahibs and I myself—ran to lift him he was dead. I helped to carry him out. Aha, he was a strong Sahib! But he is dead, and I, old Mangal Khan, am still living, by your favour.'

That was more than enough! I had my ghost—a first-hand, authenticated article. I would write to the Society for Psychical Research—I would paralyse the Empire with the news! But I would, first of all, put eighty miles of assessed crop-land between myself and that *dâk*-bungalow before nightfall. The Society might send their regular agent to investigate later on.

I went into my own room and prepared to pack, after noting down the facts of the case. As I smoked I heard the game begin again—with a miss in baulk this time, for the whir was a short one.

The door was open, and I could see into the room. *Click—click!* That was a cannon. I entered the room without fear, for there was sunlight within and a fresh breeze without. The unseen game was going on at a tremendous rate. And well it might, when a restless little rat was running to and fro inside the dingy ceiling-cloth, and a piece of loose window-sash was making fifty breaks off the window-bolt as it shook in the breeze!

Impossible to mistake the sound of billiard-balls! Impossible to mistake the whir of a ball over the slate! But I was to be excused. Even when I shut my enlightened eyes the sound was marvellously like that of a fast game.

Entered angrily the faithful partner of my sorrows, Kadir Baksh.

'This bungalow is very bad and low-caste! No wonder the Presence was disturbed and is speckled. Three sets of doolie-bearers came to the bungalow late last night when I was sleeping outside, and said that it was their custom to rest in the rooms set apart for the English people! What honour has the *khansamah*? They tried to enter, but I told them to go. No wonder, if these *Ooryas* have been here, that the Presence is sorely spotted. It is shame, and the work of a dirty man!'

Kadir Baksh did not say that he had taken from each gang two annas for rent in advance, and then, beyond my earshot, had beaten them with the big green umbrella whose use I could never before divine. But Kadir Baksh has no notions of morality.

There was an interview with the *khansamah*, but, as he promptly lost his head, wrath gave place to pity, and pity led to a long conversation, in the course of which he put the fat Engineer-Sahib's tragic death in three separate stations—two of them fifty miles away. The third shift was to Calcutta, and there the Sahib died while driving a dog-cart.

I did not go away as soon as I intended. I stayed for the night, while the wind and the rat and the sash and the window-bolt played a ding-dong hundred and fifty up. Then the wind ran out and the billiards stopped, and I felt that I had ruined my one genuine ghost story.

Had I only ceased investigating at the proper time I could have made *anything* out of it.

That was the bitterest thought of all!

The Hands of the Karma

LAFCADIO HEARN

The Japanese have as rich a tradition of ghost lore as any other nation in the world—perhaps even more so, for many of their religious and ritual ceremonies are dedicated to appeasing the spirits of those who have died. Japanese ghosts are said to appear in many different forms, the most common being dishevelled women in white robes and fierce warriors brandishing Samurai swords. These spirits are not always malevolent, but can exercise a perverse and wicked ingenuity, and they are said to frighten mainly because they bear terrible scars representing their earthly misdeeds. Other than local authorities, only one foreign writer has really managed to capture the essence of this supernatural tradition, the journalist and short story writer, Lafcadio Hearn. Hearn, the son of a British Army surgeon,

*who spent his early years living in dire poverty in America con-
tributing to small journals and local newspapers, experienced the
supernatural in both the Western world and the East. In America he
encountered ghosts in Kentucky and New Orleans (he also wrote
that he spoke to the spirit of his dead father during a seance)
and when he moved to the East to become a teacher of English,
involved himself with research into both Chinese and Japanese ghosts.
'Whoever pretends not to believe in ghosts of any sort,' he announced
later, 'lies to his own heart. Every man is haunted by ghosts.' In an
essay he published called "Of Ghosts and Goblins" he went further
and revealed one of his own experiences. 'I saw the spectre of a
woman hovering in the air above a tomb at some distance, so that I
felt safe in observing it. It had no eyes; its long hair hung loose;
its white robe floated light as smoke. I thought of a statement in a
composition by one of my pupils about ghosts. "Their greatest
peculiarity is that they have no feet!"' The result of Hearn's research
was several unique books, of which "In Ghostly Japan" is perhaps
the most outstanding and certainly now the rarest. It is from this
collection that I have extracted one of the author's own favourite and
most chilling little tales, "The Hands of the Karma".*

The daimyo's wife was dying, and knew that she was dying.
She had not been able to leave her bed since the early
autumn of the tenth Bunsei. It was now the fourth month of
the twelfth Bunsei—the year 1829 by Western counting; and
the cherry-trees were blossoming. She thought of the cherry-
trees in her garden, and of the gladness of spring. She thought
of her children. She thought of her husband's various
concubines—especially the Lady Yukiko, nineteen years old.

Editor's note: The Japanese title of this story is *Ingwa-banashi* which means
literally 'a tale of ingwa'. Ingwa is a Japanese Buddhist term for evil karma, or
evil consequence of faults committed in a former state of existence. Perhaps the
curious title is best explained by the Buddhist teaching that the dead have
power to injure the living only in consequence of evil actions committed by their
victims in some former life. Every soul is believed to have had lives before its
present existence—and will have others afterwards.

'My dear wife,' said the daimyo, 'you have suffered very much for three long years. We have done all that we could to get you well—watching beside you night and day, praying for you, and often fasting for your sake. But in spite of our loving care, and in spite of the skill of our best physicians, it would now seem that the end of your life is not far off. Probably we shall sorrow more than you will sorrow because of your having to leave what the Buddha so truly termed "this burning-house of the world". I shall order to be performed—no matter what the cost—every religious rite that can serve you in regard to your next rebirth; and all of us will pray without ceasing for you, that you may not have to wander in the Black Space, but may quickly enter Paradise, and attain to Buddhahood.'

He spoke with the utmost tenderness, caressing her the while. Then, with eyelids closed, she answered him in a voice thin as the voice of an insect:

'I am grateful—most grateful—for your kind words. . . . Yes, it is true, as you say, that I have been sick for three long years, and that I have been treated with all possible care and affection. . . . Why, indeed, should I turn away from the one true Path at the very moment of my death? . . . Perhaps to think of worldly matters at such a time is not right—but I have one last request to make—only one. . . . Call here to me the Lady Yukiko—you know that I love her like a sister. I want to speak to her about the affairs of this household.'

Yukiko came at the summons of the lord, and, in obedience to a sign from him, knelt down beside the couch. The daimyo's wife opened her eyes, and looked at Yukiko, and spoke:

'Ah, here is Yukiko! . . . I am so pleased to see you, Yukiko! . . . Come a little closer—so that you can hear me well: I am not able to speak loud. . . . Yukiko, I am going to die. I hope that you will be faithful in all things to our dear

lord—for I want you to take my place when I am gone. . . .
I hope that you will always be loved by him—yes, even a
hundred times more than I have been—and that you will
very soon be promoted to a higher rank, and become his
honoured wife. . . . And I beg of you always to cherish our
dear lord: never allow another woman to rob you of his
affection. . . . This is what I wanted to say to you, dear
Yukiko. . . . Have you been able to understand?'

'Oh, my dear Lady,' protested Yukiko, 'do not, I entreat
you, say such strange things to me! You well know that I am
of poor and mean condition—how could I ever dare to
aspire to become the wife of our lord!'

'Nay, nay!' returned the wife, huskily—'this is not a time
for words of ceremony: let us speak only the truth to each
other. After my death, you will certainly be promoted to a
higher place; and I now assure you again that I wish you to
become the wife of our lord—yes, I wish this, Yukiko,
even more than I wish to become a Buddha! . . . Ah, I had
almost forgotten!—I want you to do something for me,
Yukiko. You know that in the garden there is a *yaē-zakura*,*
which was brought here, the year before last, from Mount
Yoshino in Yamato. I have been told that it is now in full
bloom—and I wanted so much to see it in flower! In a little
while I shall be dead—I must see that tree before I die.
Now I wish you to carry me into the garden—at once,
Yukiko—so that I can see it. . . . Yes, upon your back,
Yukiko—take me upon your back. . . .'

While thus asking, her voice had gradually become clear
and strong—as if the intensity of the wish had given her new
force: then she suddenly burst into tears. Yukiko knelt
motionless, not knowing what to do; but the lord nodded
assent.

'It is her last wish in this world,' he said. 'She always

* *Yaē-zakura, yaē-no-sakura*, a variety of Japanese cherry-tree that bears
double-blossoms.

loved cherry-flowers; and I know that she wanted very much to see that Yamato-tree in blossom. Come, my dear Yukiko, let her have her will.'

As a nurse turns her back to a child, that the child may cling to it, Yukiko offered her shoulders to the wife, and said:

'Lady, I am ready: please tell me how I best can help you.'

'Why, this way!'—responded the dying woman, lifting herself with an almost super-human effort by clinging to Yukiko's shoulders. But as she stood erect, she quickly slipped her thin hands down over the shoulders, under the robe, and clutched the breasts of the girl, and burst into a wicked laugh.

'I have my wish!' she cried—'I have my wish for the cherry-bloom,* but not the cherry-bloom of the garden! . . . I could not die before I got my wish. Now I have it! —oh, what a delight!'

And with these words she fell forward upon the crouching girl, and died.

The attendants at once attempted to lift the body from Yukiko's shoulders, and to lay it upon the bed. But—strange to say!—this seemingly easy thing could not be done. The cold hands had attached themselves in some unaccountable way to the breasts of the girl—appeared to have grown into the quick flesh. Yukiko became senseless with fear and pain.

Physicians were called. They could not understand what had taken place. By no ordinary methods could the hands of the dead woman be unfastened from the body of her victim —they so clung that any effort to remove them brought blood. This was not because the fingers held: it was because the flesh of the palms had united itself in some inexplicable manner to the flesh of the breasts!

* In Japanese poetry and proverbial phraseology, the physical beauty of a woman is compared to the cherry-flower; while feminine moral beauty is compared to the plum-flower.

At that time the most skilful physician in Yedo was a foreigner—a Dutch surgeon. It was decided to summon him. After a careful examination he said that he could not understand the case, and that for the immediate relief of Yukiko there was nothing to be done except to cut the hands from the corpse. He declared that it would be dangerous to attempt to detach them from the breasts. His advice was accepted; and the hands were amputated at the wrists. But they remained clinging to the breasts; and there they soon darkened and dried up—like the hands of a person long dead.

Yet this was only the beginning of the horror.

Withered and bloodless though they seemed, those hands were not dead. At intervals they would stir—stealthily, like great grey spiders. And nightly thereafter—beginning always at the Hour of the Ox,* they would clutch and compress and torture. Only at the Hour of the Tiger the pain would cease.

Yukiko cut off her hair, and became a mendicant-nun—taking the religious name of Dassetsu. She had an *ihai* (mortuary tablet) made, bearing the *kaimyo* of her dead mistress—*Myo-Ko-In-Den Chizan-Ryo-Fu Daishi*—and this she carried about with her in all her wanderings; and every day before it she humbly besought the dead for pardon, and performed a Buddhist service in order that the jealous spirit might find rest. But the evil karma that had rendered such an affliction possible could not soon be exhausted. Every night at the Hour of the Ox, the hands never failed to torture her, during more than seventeen years—according to the testimony of those persons to whom she last told her story, when she stopped for one evening at the house of Noguchi Dengo-

* In ancient Japanese time, the Hour of the Ox was the special hour of ghosts. It began at 2 a.m., and lasted until 4 a.m.—for the old Japanese hour was double the length of the modern hour. The Hour of the Tiger began at 4 a.m.

zayémon, in the village of Tanaka in the district of Kawachi
in the province of Shimotsuké. This was in the third year of
Kokwa (1846). Thereafter nothing more was ever heard of
her.

The Monstrance

ARTHUR MACHEN

In Europe it is perhaps not surprising to find that there are a great many ghostly legends associated with war—stories of 'phantom armies' riding the skies in triumph or wearily trudging the battle-fields where they were defeated and slaughtered; tales of 'ghostly soldiers' appearing to their comrades in the trenches, and even accounts of spectre aeroplanes and tanks where no such equipment of war should be. France and Germany particularly have many such reports, not a few emanating from the terrible carnage of the First World War fought across the countryside of Western Europe. The most famous legend of the time is probably that of the 'Angels of Mons'—phantom bowmen from the time of Agincourt who allegedly came to

the rescue of beleaguered British troops during the Battle of Mons.
These spirits were said to have appeared in the skies above the
numerically superior German troops and mown them down with wave
upon wave of arrows. However, it subsequently emerged that the
story was a pure invention aimed at raising flagging British moral
back home, and had been conceived by the English journalist and
story writer, Arthur Machen. Machen published the story in
September 1914 and was then completely overwhelmed by the letters
which flooded into his newspaper both from troops at the front and
from people in Britain who insisted they had seen the bowmen or
heard absolutely reliable accounts of them. No matter how Machen
protested that it was all invention, the legend of the mysterious
archers—or Angels as they became known—found widespread
acceptance and became part of the mythology of war. Despite this
piece of imagination, Machen was a confirmed believer in the
existence of ghosts, and embodied several of his own personal
experiences as a young man in Wales into his small collection of
novels. Also, as a result of his story of the Angels of Mons, he
received details of many other supernatural incidents during the war,
and wove the following story from one case which particularly
fascinated him. It is a grim reminder of the horrors of war and of
man's inhumanity to man.

So far things were going very well indeed. The night was
thick and black and cloudy, and the German force had come
three-quarters of their way or more without an alarm. There
was no challenge from the English lines; and indeed the
English were being kept busy by a high shell-fire on their
front. This had been the German plan; and it was coming off
admirably. Nobody thought that there was any danger on
the left; and so the Prussians, writhing on their stomachs
over the ploughed field, were drawing nearer and nearer to
the wood. Once there they could establish themselves com-
fortably and securely during what remained of the night;
and at dawn the English left would be hopelessly enfiladed—
and there would be another of those movements which

people who really understand military matters call 're-adjustments of our line'.

The noise made by the men creeping and crawling over the fields was drowned by the cannonade, from the English side as well as the Germans. On the English centre and right things were indeed very brisk; the big guns were thundering and shrieking and roaring, the machine guns were keeping up the very devil's racket; the flares and illuminating shells were as good as the Crystal Palace in the old days, as the soldiers said to one another. All this had been thought of and thought out on the other side. The German force was beautifully organised. The men who crept nearer and nearer to the wood carried quite a number of machine guns in bits on their backs; others of them had small bags full of sand; yet others big bags that were empty. When the wood was reached the sand from the small bags was to be emptied into the big bags; the machine-gun parts were to be put together, the guns mounted behind the sandbag redoubt, and then, as Major Von und Zu pleasantly observed, 'the English pigs shall to gehenna-fire quickly come.'

The major was so well pleased with the way things had gone that he permitted himself a very low and guttural chuckle; in another ten minutes success would be assured. He half turned his head round to whisper a caution about some detail of the sandbag business to the big sergeant-major, Karl Heinz, who was crawling just behind him. At that instant Karl Heinz leapt into the air with a scream that rent through the night and through all the roaring of the artillery. He cried in a terrible voice, 'The Glory of the Lord!' and plunged and pitched forward, stone dead. They said that his face as he stood up there and cried aloud was as if it had been seen through a sheet of flame.

'They' were one or two out of the few who got back to the German lines. Most of the Prussians stayed in the ploughed field. Karl Heinz's scream had frozen the blood of the

English soldiers, but it had also ruined the major's plans. He and his men, caught all unready, clumsy with the burdens that they carried, were shot to pieces; hardly a score of them returned. The rest of the force were attended to by an English burying party. According to custom the dead men were searched before they were buried, and some singular relics of the campaign were found upon them, but nothing so singular as Karl Heinz's diary.

He had been keeping it for some time. It began with entries about bread and sausage and the ordinary incidents of the trenches; here and there Karl wrote about an old grandfather, and a big china pipe, and pinewoods and roast goose. Then the diarist seemed to get fidgety about his health. Thus:

'*April* 17.—Annoyed for some days by murmuring sounds in my head. I trust I shall not become deaf, like my departed uncle Christopher.

April 20.—The noise in my head grows worse; it is a humming sound. It distracts me; twice I have failed to hear the captain and have been reprimanded.

April 22.—So bad is my head that I go to see the doctor. He speaks of *tinnitus*, and gives me an inhaling apparatus that shall reach, he says, the middle ear.

April 25.—The apparatus is of no use. The sound is now become like the booming of a great church bell. It reminds me of the bell at St. Lambart on that terrible day of last August.

April 26.—I could swear that it is the bell of St. Lambart that I hear all the time. They rang it as the procession came out of the church.'

The man's writing, at first firm enough, begins to straggle unevenly over the page at this point. The entries show that he became convinced that he heard the bell of St. Lambart's Church ringing, though (as he knew better than most men) there had been no bell and no church at St. Lambart's since the summer of 1914. There was no village either—the whole place was a rubbish-heap.

Then the unfortunate Karl Heinz was beset with other troubles.

'*May* 2.—I fear I am becoming ill. To-day Joseph Kleist, who is next to me in the trench, asked me why I jerked my head to the right so constantly. I told him to hold his tongue; but this shows that I am noticed. I keep fancying that there is something white just beyond the range of my sight on the right hand.

May 3.—This whiteness is now quite clear, and in front of me. All this day it has slowly passed before me. I asked Joseph Kleist if he saw a piece of newspaper just beyond the trench. He stared at me solemnly—he is a stupid fool—and said, "There is no paper."

May 4.—It looks like a white robe. There was a strong smell of incense to-day in the trench. No one seemed to notice it. There is decidedly a white robe, and I think I can see feet, passing very slowly before me at this moment while I write.'

There is no space here for continuous extracts from Karl Heinz's diary. But to condense with severity, it would seem that he slowly gathered about himself a complete set of sensory hallucinations. First the auditory hallucination of the sound of a bell, which the doctor called *tinnitus*. Then a patch of white growing into a white robe, then the smell of incense. At last he lived in two worlds. He saw his trench, and the level before it, and the English lines; he talked with his comrades and obeyed orders, though with a certain difficulty; but he also heard the deep boom of St. Lambart's bell, and saw continually advancing towards him a white procession of little children, led by a boy who was swinging a censer. There is one extraordinary entry: 'But in August those children carried no lilies; now they have lilies in their hands. Why should they have lilies?'

It is interesting to note the transition over the border line. After May 2 there is no reference in the diary to bodily illness, with two notable exceptions. Up to and including that date the sergeant knows that he is suffering from illusions; after that he accepts his hallucinations as actualities. The man who cannot see what he sees and hear what he hears is a fool. So he writes: 'I ask who is singing "Ave Maris Stella". That blockhead Friedrich Schumacher raises his crest and answers insolently that no one sings, since singing is strictly forbidden for the present.'

A few days before the disastrous night expedition the last figure in the procession appeared to those sick eyes.

'The old priest now comes in his golden robe, the two boys holding each side of it. He is looking just as he did when he died, save that when he walked in St. Lambart there was no shining round his head. But this is illusion and contrary to reason, since no one has a shining about his head. I must take some medicine.'

Note here that Karl Heinz absolutely accepts the appearance of the martyred priest of St. Lambart as actual, while he thinks that the halo must be an illusion; and so he reverts again to his physical condition.

The priest held up both his hands, the diary states, 'as if there were something between them. But there is a sort of cloud or dimness over this object, whatever it may be. My poor Aunt Kathie suffered much from her eyes in her old age.'

One can guess what the priest of St. Lambart carried in his hands when he and the little children went out into the hot sunlight to implore mercy, while the great resounding bell of St. Lambart boomed over the plain. Karl Heinz knew what happened then; they said that it was he who killed the old priest and helped to crucify the little child against the church door. The baby was only three years old. He died calling piteously for 'mummy' and 'daddy'.

And those who will may guess what Karl Heinz saw when the mist cleared from before the monstrance in the priest's hands. Then he shrieked and died.

Escort

DAPHNE DU MAURIER

Apart from appearing in most countries of the world, there is also a long tradition of ghosts in one form or another, being witnessed at sea—I am thinking in particular of the famous old legends of phantom ships and their ghostly crews. Probably the most enduring supernatural story of this kind concerns that ghostly brigantine, 'The Flying Dutchman'. Although the origins of this legend are not too clear, it seems to have begun when a Dutch captain of ill repute was condemned, as a penalty for his sins, to sail endlessly around the Cape of Good Hope without ever being able to reach port. The only way, it is said, that the captain can expiate these sins is to make contact with another vessel and have it take a message back to his native Holland. Because such a contact is said to presage

*disaster for the ship which is approached, seamen naturally fear the
'Dutchman' and turn away at any sighting. Tales such as this one
have fascinated many writers over the years, particularly those who
live near the sea such as Daphne du Maurier, whose home is in
Cornwall. Steeped as she is in the area and its legends—such as that
of the sunken city of Lyonesse off Land's End, or the stories of
mermaids and the innumerable fables about Merlin—Miss du
Maurier has also become well aware that the ghosts of generations of
sailors who met their doom along the treacherous, rocky coast now
haunt its beautiful bays and coves. Drawing on this ambience and the
tradition of the phantom ship, she has created a compelling and
unusual tale of the supernatural at sea in "Escort".*

There is nothing remarkable about the *Ravenswing*, I can
promise you that. She is between six and seven thousand
tons, was built in 1926, and belongs to the Condor Line,
Port of Register, Hull. You can look her up in Lloyd's, if
you have a mind. There is little to distinguish her from
hundreds of other tramp steamers of her particular tonnage.
She had sailed that same route and travelled those same
waters for the three years I had served in her, and she was on
the job some time before that. No doubt she will continue
to do so for many years more and will eventually end her
days peacefully on the mud like her predecessor, the old
Gullswing, did before her; unless the U-boats get her first.

She has escaped them once, but next time we may not have
our escort. Perhaps I had better make it clear, too, that I
myself am not a fanciful man. My name is William Blunt,
and I have the reputation of living up to it. I never have
stood for nonsense of any sort, and have no time for superstition. My father was a Nonconformist minister, and maybe
that had something to do with it. I tell you this to prove my
reliability, but, for that matter, you can ask anyone in Hull.
And now, having introduced myself and the ship, I can get
on with my story.

We were homeward bound from a Scandinavian port in

the early part of the autumn. I won't give you the name of the port—the censor might stop me—but we had already made the trip there and back three times since the outbreak of war. The convoy system had not started in those first days, and the strain on the captain and myself was severe. I don't want you to infer that we were windy, or the crew either, but the North Sea in wartime is not a bed of roses, and I'll leave it at that.

When we left port that October afternoon, I could not help thinking it seemed a hell of a long way home, and it did not put me in what you would call a rollicking humour when our little Scandinavian pilot told us with a grin that a Grimsby ship, six hours ahead of us, had been sunk without warning. The Nazi government had been giving out on the wireless, he said, that the North Sea could be called the German Ocean, and the British Fleet could not do anything about it. It was all right for the pilot: he was not coming with us. He waved a cheerful farewell as he climbed over the side, and soon his boat was a black speck bobbing astern of us at the harbour entrance, and we were heading for the open sea, our course laid for home.

It was about three o'clock in the afternoon, the sea was very still and grey, and I remember thinking to myself that a periscope would not be easy to miss; at least we would have fair warning, unless the glass fell and it began to blow. However, it did the nerves no good to envisage something that was not going to happen, and I was pretty short with the first engineer when he started talking about the submarine danger, and why the hell did not the Admiralty do something about it?

'Your job is to keep the old *Ravenswing* full steam ahead for home and beauty, isn't it?' I said. 'If Winston Churchill wants your advice, no doubt he'll send for you.' He had no answer to that, and I lit my pipe and went on to the bridge to take over from the captain.

I suppose I'm not out-of-the-way observant about my

fellow men, and I certainly did not notice then that there was anything wrong with the captain. He was never much of a talker at any time. The fact that he went to his cabin at once meant little or nothing. I knew he was close at hand if anything unusual should happen.

It turned very cold, after nightfall, and later a thin rain began to fall. The ship rolled slightly as she met the longer seas. The sky was overcast with the rain, and there were no stars. The autumn nights are always black, of course, in northern waters, but this night the darkness seemed intensified. There would be small chance of sighting a periscope, I thought, under these conditions, and it might well be that we should receive no other intimation than the shock of the explosion. Someone said the other day that the U-boats carried a new type of torpedo, supercharged, and that explained why the ships attacked sank so swiftly.

The *Ravenswing* would founder in three or four minutes if she was hit right amidships and it might be that we should never even sight the craft that sank us. The submarine would vanish in the darkness; they would not bother to pick up survivors. They could not see them if they wanted to, not in this darkness. I glanced at the chap at the wheel, he was a little Welshman from Cardiff, and he had a trick of sucking his false teeth and clicking them back again every few minutes. We stood a pretty equal chance, he and I, standing side by side together on the bridge. It was then I turned suddenly and saw the captain standing in the entrance to his cabin. He was holding on for support, his face was very flushed, and he was breathing heavily.

'Is anything wrong, sir?' I said.

'This damn pain in my side,' he gasped; 'started it yesterday, and thought I'd strained myself. Now I'm doubled up with the bloody thing. Got any aspirin?'

Aspirin my foot, I thought. If he has not got acute appendicitis, I'll eat my hat. I'd seen a man attacked like that before; he'd been rushed to a hospital and operated

on in less than two hours. They'd taken an appendix out of
him swollen as big as a fist.

'Have you a thermometer there?' I asked the captain.

'Yes,' he said. 'What the hell's the use of that? I haven't
got a temperature. I've strained myself, I tell you. I want
some aspirin.'

I took his temperature. It was a hundred and four. The
sweat was pouring down his forehead. I put my hand on his
stomach, and it was rigid, like a brick wall. I helped him to
his berth and covered him up with blankets. Then I made
him drink half a glass of brandy neat. It may be the worst
thing you can do for appendicitis, but when you are hundreds
of miles from a surgeon and in the middle of the North Sea
in wartime you are apt to take chances.

The brandy helped to dull the pain a little, and that was
the only thing that mattered. Whatever the result to the
captain, it had but one result for me. I was in command of
the *Ravenswing* from now on, and mine was the responsibility of bringing her home through those submarine-
infested waters. I, William Blunt, had got to see this through.

It was bitter cold. All feeling had long since left my hands
and feet. I was conscious of a dull pain in those parts of my
body where my hands and feet should have been. But the
effect was curiously impersonal. The pain might have
belonged to someone else, the sick captain himself even,
back there in his cabin, lying moaning and helpless as I
had left him last, some forty-eight hours before. He was not
my charge; I could do nothing for him. The steward nursed
him with brandy and aspirin, and I remember feeling
surprised, in a detached sort of way, that he did not die.

'You ought to get some sleep. You can't carry on like this.
Why don't you get some sleep?'

Sleep. That was the trouble. What was I doing at that
moment but rocking on my two feet on the borderline of
oblivion, with the ship in my charge, and this voice in my
left ear the sound that brought me to my senses. It was

Carter, the second mate. His face looked pinched and anxious.

'Supposing you get knocked up?' he was saying. 'What am I going to do? Why don't you think of me?'

I told him to go to hell, and stamped down the bridge to bring the life back to my numbed feet, and to disguise the fact from Carter that sleep had nearly been victorious.

'What else do you think has kept me on the bridge for forty-eight hours but the thought of you,' I said, 'and the neat way you let the stern hawser drop adrift, with the second tug alongside, last time we were in Hull? Get me a cup of tea and a sandwich and shut your bloody mouth,' I said.

My words must have relieved him, for he grinned back at me and shot down the ladder like a Jack-in-the-box. I held on to the bridge and stared ahead, sweeping the horizon for what seemed like the hundred thousandth time, and seeing always the same blank face of the sea, slate grey and still. There were low-banked clouds to the westward, whether mist or rain I could not tell, but they gathered slowly without wind and the glass held steady, while there was a certain smell about the air, warning of fog. I swallowed my cup of tea and made short work of a sandwich, and I was feeling in my pocket for my pipe and a box of matches when the thing happened for which, I suppose, I had consciously been training myself since the captain went sick some forty-eight hours before.

'Object to port. Three-quarters of a mile distant. Looks like a periscope.'

The words came from the lookout on the fo'c'sle head, and so flashed back to the watch on deck. As I snatched my glasses I caught a glimpse of the faces of the men lining the ship's side, curiously uniform they were, half eager, half defiant.

Yes. There she was. No doubt now. A thin grey line, like a needle away there on our port bow, leaving a narrow wake

behind her like a jagged ripple. Once again I was aware of
Carter beside me, tense, expectant, and I noticed that his
hands trembled slightly as he lifted the glasses in his turn. I
gave the necessary alteration of our course, and telegraphed
the corresponding change of speed down to the first engineer,
and then took up my glasses once more. The change of
course had brought the periscope right ahead, and for a
few minutes or so the thin line continued on its way as
though indifferent to our manœuvre, and then, as I had
feared and foreseen, the submarine altered course, even as
we had done, and the periscope bore down upon us, this
time to starboard.

'She's seen us,' said Carter.

'Yes,' I said. He looked up at me, his brown eyes troubled
like a spaniel puppy's. We altered course again and increased
out speed, this time bringing our stern to the thin grey
needle, so that for a moment it seemed as though the gap
between us would be widened and she would pass away
behind us, but, swift and relentless, she bore up again on
our quarter, and little Carter began to swear, fluently and
passionately, the futility of words a sop to his own fear. I
sympathised, seeing in a flash, as the proverbial drowning
man is said to do, an episode in my own childhood when my
father lectured me for lying, and even as I remembered
this picture of a long-forgotten past I spoke down the
mouth tube to the engine-room once more and ordered yet
another alteration in our speed.

The watch below had now all hurriedly joined the watch
on deck. They lined the side of the ship, as though hyp-
notised by that unwavering grey line that crept closer, ever
closer.

'She's breaking surface,' said Carter. 'Watch that line of
foam.'

The periscope had come abeam of us and had drawn
ahead. It was now a little over a mile distant, on our port
bow. Carter was right. She was breaking surface, even as he

said. We could see the still water become troubled and disturbed and then slowly, inevitably, the squat conning tower appeared and the long, lean form rose from the depths like a black slug, the water streaming from its decks.

'The bastards,' whispered Carter to himself: 'the filthy, stinking bastards.'

The men clustered together below me on the deck watched the submarine with a strange indifference, like spectators at some show with which they had no concern. I saw one fellow point out some technical detail of the submarine to the man by his side; and then light a cigarette. His companion laughed, and spat over the side of the ship into the water. I wondered how many of them could swim.

I gave the final order through to the engine-room, and then ordered all hands on deck, to boat stations. My next order would depend on the commander of the submarine.

'They'll shell the boats,' said Carter, 'they won't let us get away, they'll shell the boats.'

'Oh, for God's sake,' I began, the pallor of his face begetting in me a furious senseless anger, when suddenly I caught sight of the wall of fog that was rolling down upon us from astern. I swung Carter round by the shoulders to meet it. 'Look there,' I said, 'look there,' and his jaw dropped, and he grinned stupidly. Already the visibility around us was no more than a cable's length on either side, and the first drifting vapour stung us with its cold, sour smell. Above us the air was thick and clammy. In a moment our after shrouds were lost to sight. I heard one fellow strike up the opening chorus of a comic song in a high falsetto voice, and he was immediately cursed to silence by his companions. Ahead of us lay the submarine, dark and immobile, the water still running from its sides, the decks as yet unmanned, and her long snout caught unexpectedly in a sudden shaft of light. Then the white fog that enveloped us crept forward and beyond, the sky descended, and our world was blotted out.

It wanted two minutes to midnight, I crouched low under cover of the bridge and flashed a torch on to my watch. No bell had been sounded since the submarine had first been sighted, some eight hours earlier. We waited. Darkness had travelled with the fog, and night fell early. There was silence everywhere, but for the creaking of the ship as she rolled in the swell and the thud of water slapping her sides as she lay over, first on one side, then on the other. Still we waited. The cold was no longer so intense as it had been. There was a moist, clammy feeling in the air. The men talked in hushed whispers beneath the bridge. We went on waiting. Once I entered the cabin where the captain lay sick, and flashed my torch on to him. His face was flushed and puffy. His breathing was heavy and slow. He was sleeping fitfully, moaning now and again, and once he opened his eyes, but he did not recognise me. I went back to the bridge. The fog had lifted slightly, and I could see our forward shrouds and the fo'c'sle head. I went down on to the deck and leant over the ship's side. The tide was running strongly to the south. It had turned three hours before, and for the fourth time that evening I began to calculate our drift. I was turning to the ladder to climb to the bridge once more, when I heard footsteps running along the deck, and a man cannonaded into me.

'Fog's lifting astern,' he said breathlessly, 'and there's something coming up on our starboard quarter.'

I ran back along the deck with him. A group of men were clustered at the ship's side, talking eagerly. 'It's a ship all right, sir,' said one. 'Looks like a Finnish barque. I can see her canvas.'

I peered into the darkness with them. Yes, there she was, about a hundred yards distant, and bearing down upon us. A great three-masted vessel, with a cloud of canvas aloft. It was too late in the year for the grain ships. What the hell was she doing in these waters in wartime? Unless she was carrying timber. Had she seen us, though? That was the point. Here we were, without lights, skulking in the trough of the sea because of that damned submarine, and now risking almost certain collision with some old timber ship.

If only I could be certain that the tide and the fog had put up a number of miles between us and the enemy. She was coming up fast, the old-timer, God knows where she found her wind—there was none on my left cheek that would blow out a candle. If she passed us at this rate there would be fifty yards to spare, no more, and with that hell ship waiting yonder in the darkness somewhere, the Finn would go straight to kingdom come.

'All right,' I said, 'she's seen us; she's bearing away.' I could only make out her outline in the darkness as she travelled past abeam. A great, high-sided vessel she was, in ballast probably, or there would never have been so much of her out of the water. I'd forgotten they had such bulky afterdecks. Her spars were not the clean things I remembered either; these were a mass of rigging, and the yards an extraordinary length, necessary, no doubt, for all that bunch of canvas.

'She's not going to pass us,' said somebody, and I heard the blocks rattle and jump, and the rigging slat, as the great yards swung over. And was that faint high note, curious and immeasurably distant, the pipe of a boatswain's whistle? But the fog vapour was drifting down on us again, and the ship was hidden. We strained our eyes in the darkness, seeing nothing, and I was about to turn back to the bridge again when a thin call came to us across the water.

'Are you in distress?' came the hail. Whether her nationality was Finnish or not, at least her officer spoke good English, even if his phrasing was a little unusual. I was wary though, and I did not answer. There was a pause, and then the voice travelled across to us once more. 'What ship are you, and where are you bound?'

And then, before I could stop him, one of our fellows bellowed out: 'There's an enemy submarine come to the surface about half a mile ahead of us.' Someone smothered the idiot half a minute too late and, for better or worse, our flag had been admitted.

We waited. None of us moved a finger. All was silent. Presently we heard the splash of oars and the low murmur of voices. They were sending a boat across to us from the barque. There was something furtive and strange about the whole business. I was suspicious. I did not like it. I felt for the hard butt of my revolver, and was reassured. The sound of oars drew nearer. A long, low boat like a West Country gig drew out of the shadows, manned by half a dozen men. There was a fellow with a lantern in the bows. Someone, an officer I presumed, stood up in the stern. It was too dark for me to see his face. The boat pulled up beneath us, and the men rested on their oars.

'Captain's compliments, gentlemen, and do you desire an escort?' inquired the officer.

'What the hell!' began one of our men, but I cursed him to quiet. I leaned over the side, shading my eyes from the light of the boat's lantern.

'Who are you?' I said.

'Lieutenant Arthur Mildmay, at your service, sir,' replied the voice.

There was nothing foreign in his intonation. I could swear to that, but again I was struck by his phraseology. No snottie in the Navy ever talked like this. The Admiralty might have bought up a Finnish barque, of course, and armed her, like Von Luckner did in the last war, but the idea seemed unlikely.

'Are you camouflaged?' I asked.

'I beg your pardon?' he replied in some surprise. Then his English was not so fluent as I thought. Once again I felt for my revolver. 'You're not trying to make a fool of me by any chance, are you?' I said sarcastically.

'Not in the least,' replied the voice. 'I repeat the captain sends his compliments, and as you gave him to understand

we are in the immediate vicinity of the enemy, he desires
me to offer you his protection. Our orders are to escort any
merchant ships we find to a port of safety.'

'And who issued those orders?' I said.

'His Majesty King George, of course,' replied the voice.

It was then, I think, that I felt for the first time a curious
chill of fear. I remember swallowing hard. My threat felt
dry, and I could not answer at once. I looked at the men
around me, and they wore, one and all, a silly, dumb,
unbelieving expression on their faces.

'He says the King sent him,' said the fellow beside me, and
then his voice trailed away uncertainly, and he fell silent.

I heard Carter tap me on the shoulder, 'Send them away,'
he whispered. 'There's something wrong; it's a trap.'

The man kneeling in the bows of the gig flashed his
lantern in my face, blinding me. The young lieutenant
stepped across the thwarts and took the lantern from him.
'Why not come aboard and speak to the captain yourself, if
you are in doubt?' he said.

Still I could not see his face, but he wore some sort of
cloak round his shoulders, and the hand that held the
lantern was long and slim. The lantern that dazzled me
brought a pain across my eyes so severe that for a few
moments I could neither speak nor think, and then, to my
own surprise, I heard myself answer: 'Very well, make room
for me, then, in your boat.'

Carter laid his hand on my arm.

'You're crazy,' he said. 'You can't leave the ship.'

I shook him off, obstinate for no reason, determined on
my venture. 'You're in charge, Carter,' I said. 'I shan't be
long away. Let me go, you damn' fool.'

I ordered the ladder over the side, and wondered, with a
certain irritation, why the stupid fellows gaped at me as they
obeyed. I had that funny reckless feeling that comes upon
you when you're half drunk, and I wondered if the reason
for it was my own lack of sleep for over forty-eight hours.

I landed with a thud in the gig, and stumbled to the stern beside the officer. The men bent on their oars, and the boat began to creep across the water to the barque. It was bitter cold. The clammy mugginess was gone. I turned up the collar of my coat and tried to catch a closer glimpse of my companion, but it was black as pitch in the boat and his features were completely hidden from me.

I felt the seat under me, with my hand. It was like ice, freezing to the touch and I plunged my hands deep in my pockets. The cold seemed to penetrate my greatcoat, and find my flesh. My teeth chattered, and I could not stop them. The chap in front of me, bending to his oar, was a great burly brute, with shoulders like an ox. His sleeves were rolled up above his elbows, his arms were bare. He was whistling softly between his teeth.

'You don't feel the cold, then?' I asked.

He did not answer, and I leant forward and looked into his face. He stared at me, as though I did not exist, and went on whistling between his teeth. His eyes were deep set, sunken in his head. His checkbones were very prominent and high. He wore a queer, stovepipe of a hat, shiny and black.

'Look here,' I said, tapping him on his knee, 'I'm not here to be fooled, I can tell you that.'

And then the lieutenant, as he styled himself, stood up beside me in the stern. 'Ship ahoy,' he called, his two hands to his mouth, and looking up, I saw we were already beneath the barque, her great sides towering above us. A lantern appeared on the bulwark by the ladder, and again my eyes were dazzled by the sickly yellow light.

The lieutenant swung on to the ladder, and I followed him, hand over fist, breathing hard, for the bitter cold caught at me and seemed to strike right down into my throat. I paused when I reached the deck, with a stitch in my side like a kicking horse, and in that queer half-light that came from the flickering lanterns I saw that this was no

Finnish barque with a load of timber, no grain ship in ballast, but a raider bristling with guns. Her decks were cleared for action, and the men were there ready at their stations. There was much activity and shouting, and a voice from for'ard calling out orders in a thin high voice.

There seemed to be a haze of smoke thick in the air, and a heavy sour stench, and with it all the cold dank chill I could not explain.

'What is it?' I called. 'What's the game?' No one answered. Figures passed me and brushed me, shouting and laughing at one another. A lad of about thirteen ran by me, with a short blue jacket and long white trousers, while close beside me, crouching by his gun, was a great bearded fellow like my oarsman of the gig, with a striped stocking cap upon his head. Once again, above the hum and confusion, I heard the thin, shrill piping of the boatswain's whistle and, turning, I saw a crowd of jostling men running barefooted to the afterdeck, and I caught the gleam of steel in their hands.

'The captain will see you, if you come aft,' said the lieutenant.

I followed him, angry and bewildered. Carter was right, I had been fooled; and yet as I stumbled in the wake of the lieutenant I heard English voices shouting on the deck, and funny unfamiliar English oaths.

We pushed through the door of the afterdeck, and the musty rank smell became more sour and more intense. It was darker still. Blinking, I found myself at the entrance of a large cabin, lit only by flickering lantern light, and in the centre of the cabin was a long table, and a man was sitting there in a funny high-backed chair. Three or four other men stood behind him, but the lantern light shone on his face alone. He was very thin, very pale, and his hair was ashen grey, I saw by the patch he wore that he had lost the sight of one eye, but the other eye looked through me in the cold abstracted way of someone who would get his business done, and has little time to spare.

'Your name, my man?' he said, tapping with his hand upon the table before him.

'William Blunt, sir,' I said, and I found myself standing to attention, with my cap in my hands, my throat as dry as a bone, and that same funny chill of fear in my heart.

'You report there is an enemy vessel close at hand, I understand?'

'Yes, sir,' I said. 'A submarine came to the surface about a mile distant from us, some hours ago. She had been following us for half an hour before she broke surface. Luckily the fog came down and hid us. That was at about half-past four in the afternoon. Since then we have not attempted to steam, but have drifted without lights.'

He listened to me in silence. The figures behind him did not move. There was something sinister in their immobility and his, as though my words meant nothing to them, as though they did not believe me or did not understand.

'I shall be glad to offer you my assistance, Mr. Blunt,' he said at last. I stood awkwardly, still turning my cap in my hands. He did not mean to make game of me, I realised that, but what use was his ship to me?

'I don't quite see,' I began, but he held up his hand. 'The enemy will not attack you while you are under my protection,' he said; 'if you care to accept my escort, I shall be very pleased to give you safe-conduct to England. The fog has lifted, and luckily the wind is with us.'

I swallowed hard. I did not know what to say.

'We steam at eleven knots,' I said awkwardly, and when he did not reply I stepped forward to his table, thinking he had not heard.

'Supposing the blighter is still there?' I said. 'He'll get the pair of us. She'll blow up like matchwood, this ship of yours. You stand even less chance than us.'

The man seated by the table leant back in his chair. I saw

him smile. 'I've never run from a Frenchman yet,' he said.

Once again I heard the boatswain's whistle, and the patter of bare feet overhead upon the deck. The lanterns swayed, in a current of air from the swinging door. The cabin seemed very musty, very dark. I felt faint and queer, and something like a sob rose in my throat which I could not control.

'I'd like your escort,' I stammered, and even as I spoke he rose in his chair and leant towards me. I saw the faded blue of his coat, and the ribbon across it. I saw his pale face very close, and the one blue eye. I saw him smile, and I felt the strength of the hand that held mine and saved me from falling.

They must have carried me to the boat and down the ladder, for when I opened my eyes again, with a queer dull ache at the back of my head, I was at the foot of my own gangway, and my own chaps were hauling me aboard. I could just hear the splash of oars as the gig pulled away back to the barque.

'Thank God you're back!' said Carter. 'What the devil did they do to you. You're as white as chalk. Were they Finns or Boche?'

'Neither,' I said curtly; 'they're English, like ourselves. I saw the captain. I've accepted his escort home.'

'Have you gone raving mad?' said Carter.

I did not answer, I went up to the bridge and gave orders for steaming. Yes, the fog was lifting, and above my head I could see the first pale glimmer of a star. I listened, well content, to the familiar noises of the ship as we got under way again. The throb of the screw, the thrash of the propeller. The relief was tremendous. No more silence, no more inactivity. The strain was broken, and the men were themselves again, cheerful, cracking jokes at one another. The cold had vanished, and the curious dead fatigue that had been part of my mind and body for so long. The warmth was coming back to my hands and my feet.

Slowly we began to draw ahead once more, ploughing our way in the swell, while to starboard of us, some hundred yards distant, came our escort, the white foam hissing from her bows, her cloud of canvas billowing to a wind that none of us could feel. I saw the helmsman beside me glance at her out of the tail of his eye, and when he thought I was not looking he wet his finger and held it in the air. Then his eye met mine, and fell again, and he whistled a song to show he did not care. I wondered if he thought me as mad as Carter did. Once I went in to see the captain. The steward was with him, and when I entered he switched on the lamp above the captain's berth.

'His fever's down,' he said. 'He's sleeping naturally at last. I don't think we're going to lose him, after all.'

'No, I guess he'll be all right,' I said.

I went back to the bridge, whistling the song I had heard from the sailor in the gig. It was a jaunty, lilting tune, familiar in a rum sort of way, but I could not put a name to it. The fog had cleared entirely, and the sky was ablaze with stars. We were steaming now at our full rate of knots, but still our escort kept abeam, and sometimes, if anything, she drew just a fraction ahead.

Whether the submarine was on the surface still, or whether she had dived, I neither knew nor cared, for I was full of that confidence that I had lacked before and which, after a while, seemed to possess the helmsman in his turn, so that he grinned at me, jerking his head at our escort, and said, 'There don't seem to be no flies on Nancy, do there?' and fell, as I did, to whistling that nameless jaunty tune. Only Carter remained sullen and aloof. His fear had given way to sulky silence, and at last, sick of the sight of his moody face staring through the chartroom window, I ordered him below, and was aware of a new sense of freedom and relief when he had gone.

So the night wore on, and we, plunging and rolling in the wake of our escort, saw never a sight of periscope or lean grey hull again. At last the sky lightened to the eastward, and low down on the horizon appeared the streaky pallid dawn. Five bells struck, and away ahead of us, faint as a whisper, came the answering pipe of a boatswain's whistle. I think I was the one that heard it. Then I heard the weak, tired voice of the captain calling me from his cabin. I went to him at once. He was propped up against his pillows, and I could tell from his face he was as weak as a rat, but his temperature was normal, even as the steward had said.

'Where are we, Blunt?' he said. 'What's happened?'

'We'll be safely berthed before the people ashore have rung for breakfast,' I said. 'The coast's ahead of us now.'

'What's the date, man?' he asked. I told him.

'We've made good time,' he said. I agreed.

'I shan't forget what you've done, Blunt,' he said. 'I'll speak to the owners about you. You'll be getting promotion for this.'

'Promotion my backside,' I said. 'It's not me that needs thanking, but our escort away on the starboard bow.'

'Escort?' he said, staring at me. 'What escort? Are we travelling with a bloody convoy?'

Then I told him the story, starting with the submarine, and the fog, and so on to the coming of the barque herself, and my own visit aboard her, and not missing out an account of my own nerves and jumpiness, either. He listened to me, dazed and bewildered on his pillow.

'What's the name of your barque?' he said slowly, when I had finished.

I smote my hand on my knee. 'It may be Old Harry for all I know; I never asked them,' I said, and I began whistling the tune that the fellow had sung as he bent to his oars in the gig.

'I can't make it out,' said the captain; 'you know as well as I do there aren't any sailing ships left on the British register.'

I shrugged my shoulders. Why the hell couldn't he accept the escort as naturally as I and the men had done?

'Get me a drink, and stop whistling that confounded jig,' said the captain. I laughed, and gave him his glass.

'What's wrong with it?' I said.

'It's "Lilliburlero", centuries old. What makes you whistle that?' he said. I stared back at him, and I was not laughing any longer.

'I don't know,' I said, 'I don't know.'

He drank thirstily, watching me over the rim of his glass. 'Where's your precious escort now?' he said.

'On the starboard bow,' I repeated, and I went forward to the bridge again and gazed seaward, where I knew her to be.

The sun, like a great red globe, was topping the horizon, and the night clouds were scudding to the west. Far ahead lay the coast of England. But our escort had gone.

I turned to the fellow steering. 'When did she go?' I asked.

'Beg pardon, sir?' he said.

'The sailing ship. What's happened to her?' I repeated.

The man looked puzzled, and cocked his eye at me curiously.

'I've seen no sailing ship,' he said. 'There's a destroyer been abeam of us some time. She must have come up with us under cover of darkness. I've only noticed her since the sun rose.'

I snatched up my glasses and looked to the west. The fellow was not dreaming. There was a destroyer with us, as he said. She plunged into the long seas, churning up the water and chucking it from her like a great white wall of foam. I watched her for a few minutes in silence, and then I lowered my glasses. The fellow steering gazed straight in front of him. Now daylight had come he seemed changed in a queer, indefinable way. He no longer whistled jauntily. He was his usual stolid seaman self.

'We shall be docked by nine-thirty. We've made good time,' I said.

'Yes, sir,' he said.

Already I could see a black dot far ahead, and a wisp of smoke. The tugs were lying off for us. Carter was in my old place on the fo'c'sle head. The men were at their stations. I, on the captain's bridge, would bring his ship to port. He called me to him, five minutes before the tugs took us in tow, when the first gulls were wheeling overhead.

'Blunt,' he said, 'I've been thinking. That captain fellow you spoke to in the night, on board that sailing craft. You say he wore a black patch over one eye. Did he by any chance have an empty sleeve pinned to his breast as well?'

I did not answer. We looked at one another in silence. Then a shrill whistle warned me that the pilot's boat was alongside. Somewhere, faint and far, the echo sounded like a boatswain's pipe.

South Sea Bubble

HAMMOND INNES

While phantom ships like 'The Flying Dutchman' are comparatively rare, modern vessels that are haunted by the spirits of dead captains or crew members occur rather more frequently. These vessels can range from ocean-going liners where the spectral form of a departed chief officer walks the bridge during the 'dog hours', to a small pleasure boat haunted by the shade of an amateur sailor who was drowned in mysterious circumstances. As readers of sea stories will know already, there are few better modern writers in this genre than Hammond Innes, who has based most of his best-selling novels on personal experience mixed with exhaustive research. He describes his own encounter with the supernatural in the following story. "South Sea Bubble" vividly captures the feeling of being at sea in the

*company of a strange and dangerous companion not of this world. . . .
To say more here would spoil your enjoyment of the tale. Mr Innes
wrote "South Sea Bubble" especially for publication at Christmas
which, as I said in my Introduction, is the time when the British
particularly enjoy a good ghost story. After reading it we can then
pass quite naturally on to the date which the Americans especially
reserve for celebration of the supernormal, Hallowe'en.*

She lay in Kinlochbervie in the north-west of Scotland, so
cheap I should have known there was something wrong. I
had come by way of Lairg, under the heights of Arkle, and
four miles up the road that skirts the north shores of Loch
Laxford I turned a corner and there she was—a ketch
painted black and lying to her own reflection in the evening
sun.

Dreams, dreams . . . dreams are fine, as an escape, as a
means of counteracting the pressures of life in a big office.
But when there is no barrier between dream and reality,
what then? Draw back, create another dream? But one is
enough for any man and this had been mine; that one day I
would find the boat of my dream and sail her to the South
Seas.

Maybe it was the setting, the loneliness of the loch, the aid
of Nordic wildness with the great humped hills of Sutherland
as backcloth and the mass of Arkle cloud-capped in splend-
our. Here the Vikings had settled. From here men only just
dead sailed open boats south for the herring. Even her name
seemed right—*Samoa.*

I bought her, without a survey, without stopping to think.
And then my troubles started.

She was dry when I bought her. Nobody told me the
agents had paid a man to pump her out each day. If my
wife had been alive I would never have been such a fool. But
it was an executor's sale. The agents told me that. Also that
she had been taken in tow off Handa Island by a Fraser-
burgh trawler and was the subject of a salvage claim. With

her port of registry Kingston, Jamaica, it explained the low asking price. What they didn't tell me was that the trawler had found her abandoned, drifting water-logged without a soul on board. Nor did they tell me that her copper sheathing was so worn that half her underwater planking was rotten with toredo.

'A wee bit of a mystery,' was the verdict of the crofter who helped me clean her up and pump the water out of her. Nobody seemed to know who had sailed her across the Atlantic, how many had been on board, or what had happened to them.

The first night I spent on board—I shall always remember that; the excitement, the thrill of ownership, of command, of being on board a beautiful ship that was also now my home. The woodwork gleamed in the lamplight (yes, she had oil lamps as well as electric light), and lying in the quarter berth I could look up through the open hatch to the dark shape of the hills black against the stars. I was happy in spite of everything, happier than I had been for a long time, and when I finally went to sleep it was with a picture of coral islands in my mind—white sands and palm trees and proas scudding across the pale green shallows of warm lagoons.

I woke shivering, but not with cold. It was a warm night and the cold was inside me. I was cold to my guts and very frightened. It wasn't the strangeness of my new habitation, for I knew where I was the instant I opened my eyes. And it wasn't fear of the long voyage ahead. It was something else, something I didn't understand.

I shifted to one of the saloon berths, and as I slept soundly the rest of the night I put it down to nerves. It was a nervous breakdown that had led to my early retirement, enabling me to exchange my small suburban house for the thing I had always dreamed of. But I avoided the quarter berth after that, and though I was so tired every night that I fell asleep almost instantly, a sense of uneasiness persisted.

It is difficult to describe, even more difficult to explain.

There was no repetition of the waking cold of that first night, but every now and then I had the sense of a presence on board. It was so strong at times that when I came back from telephoning or collecting parts or stores I would find myself looking about me as though expecting somebody to be waiting for me.

There was so much to do, and so little time, that I never got around to making determined inquiries as to whether the previous owner had been on that ill-fated voyage. I did write to his address in Kingston, but with no reply I was left with a sense of mystery and the feeling that whatever it was that had happened, it had become imprinted on the fabric of the boat. How else to explain the sense of somebody, something, trying to communicate?

It was August when I bought her, late September when I sailed out of Kinlochbervie bound for Shetland. It would have been more sensible to have headed south to an English yard, for my deadline to catch the trades across the Atlantic was December. But Scalloway was cheaper. And nearer.

I left with a good forecast, and by nightfall I was motoring north in a flat calm with Cape Wrath light bearing 205° and beginning to dip below the dark line of the horizon. My plan to install larger batteries, an alternator and an automatic pilot had had to be shelved. The money for that was now earmarked for new planking. I stayed on deck, dozing at the helm and watching for trawlers. I was tired before I started and I was tireder now.

A hand touched my shoulder and I woke with a start to complete silence. It was pitch dark, clammily cold. For a moment I couldn't think where I was. Then I saw the shadowy outline of the mainsail above my head. Nothing else—no navigation lights, no compass light, the engine stopped and the boat sluggish. I switched on my torch and the beam shone white on fog. The sails, barely visible, were drawing and we were moving slowly westward, out into the Atlantic.

I pressed the self-starter, but nothing happened, and when I put the wheel over she took a long time to come back on course. I went below then and stepped into a foot or more of water. Fortunately I had installed a powerful, double-action pump. Even so, it took me the better part of four hours to get the water level below the cabin sole. By then it was daylight and the fog had cleared away to the west, a long bank of it looking like a smudge of smoke as the sun glimmered through the damp air.

I tried swinging the engine, but it was no good. Just as well perhaps, because it must have been the prolonged running of the engine that had caused her to take in so much water. Without it the leaks in the planking seemed no worse than when she had been at anchor. I cooked myself a big breakfast on the paraffin stove and it was only when I was sitting over coffee and a cigarette that I remembered how I had woken to the feel of a hand on my shoulder.

I put it out of my mind, not wanting to know about it, and switched to consideration of whether to go on or turn back. But I was already nearly halfway to Shetland and the wind settled the matter by coming from the south-west. I eased sheets and for the next hour we were sailing at almost 6 knots.

The wind held steady all day at Force 3–4, and though there were occasional fog patches I did manage to catch a glimpse of Orkney away to the south-east. Sail trimming and pumping took most of my time, but in the afternoon, when the pump at last sucked dry. I was able to give some thought to navigation.

The tides run strong in the waters between Orkney and Shetland, up to 10 knots in the vicinity of the major headlands, and I had an uneasy feeling I was being carried too far to the east. Just before midnight I sighted what looked like the loom of a light almost over the bows, but my eyes were too tired to focus clearly. I pumped until the bilges sucked dry again, checked the compass and the log, then fell into the quarter berth, still with my oilskins on, not caring whether it was a light or a ship, or whether the boat held her course or not.

I was utterly exhausted and I came out of a dead sleep to see the shadowy figure of a man standing over me. He had something in his hand, and as his arm came up, I rolled off the bunk, hit the floorboards and came up crouched, the hair on my neck prickling, my body trembling.

Maybe I dreamed it; there was nothing there, and the only sound on board the slatting of the sails. But still my body trembled and I was cold with fright. I had a slug of whisky and went up on deck to find the log line hanging inert, the ship drifting in circles; no wind and the fog like a wet shroud.

I stayed on deck until it got light—a ghostly, damp morning, everything dripping. I pumped the bilges dry, cooked breakfast, attended to the navigation. But though I was fully occupied, I couldn't get it out of my head that I wasn't alone on the ship. Now, whatever I was doing, wherever I was on the boat, I was conscious of his presence.

I know I was tired. But why had my reflexes been so instantaneous? How had I known in the instant of waking that the man standing over me was bent on murder?

The day dragged, the wind coming and going, my world enclosed in walls of fog. The circle of sea in which I was imprisoned was never still, enlarging and contracting with the varying density of the fog, and it was cold. Hot tea, exercise, whisky—nothing seemed to dispel that cold. It was deep inside me, a brooding fear.

But of what?

Shetland was getting close now. I knew it would be a tricky landfall, in fog and without an engine. The tidal stream, building up against the long southern finger of the islands, causes one of the worst races in the British Isles. Roost is the local name and the Admiralty Pilot warned particularly of the roost off Sumburgh Head. It would only require a small error of navigation. . . . And then, dozing at the helm, I thought I saw two figures in the bows.

I jerked awake, my vision blurred with moisture, seeing them vaguely. But when I rubbed my eyes they were gone. And just before dusk, when I was at the mainmast checking the halyards, I could have sworn there was somebody standing behind me. The fog, tiredness, hallucinations— it is easy not to rationalise. But the ever-present feeling that I was not alone on the boat, the sense of fear, of something terrible hanging over me—that's not so easy to explain.

Night fell, the breeze died and the damp blanket of fog clamped down. I could feel the wetness of it on my eyeballs, my oilskins clammy with moisture and water dripping off the boom as though it were raining. I pumped the bilges dry and had some food. When I came up on deck again there was the glimmer of a moon low down, the boat's head swinging slowly in an eddy. And then I heard it, to the north of me, the soft mournful note of a diaphone—the fog signal on Sumburgh Head.

The tide had just started its main south-easterly flow and within an hour the roost was running and I was in it. The sea became lumpy, full of unpredictable hollows. Sudden overfalls reared up and broke against the top-sides. The movement grew and became indescribable, exhausting, and above the noise of water breaking, the sound of the sails slatting back and forth.

I was afraid of the mast then. I had full main and genoa up. I don't know how long it took me to get the headsail down and lashed, the boat like a mad thing intent on pitching me overboard. An hour maybe. And then the main. I couldn't lash it properly, the movement of the boom too violent. Blood was dripping from a gash in my head where I had been thrown against a winch, my body a mass of bruises. I left the mainsail heaped on deck and wedged myself into the quarter berth. It was the only safe place, the saloon a shambles of crockery and stores, locker doors swinging, the contents flying.

I was scared. The movement was so violent I couldn't pump. I couldn't do anything. I must have passed out from sheer exhaustion when I suddenly saw again the figure standing over the quarter berth, and the thing in his hand was a winch handle. I was seeing it vaguely now, as though from a long way away. I saw the man's arm come up. The metal of the winch handle gleamed. I saw him strike, and as he struck the figure in the bunk moved, rolling out on to the floorboards and coming up in a crouch, his head gashed and blood streaming. There was fear there. I can remember fear then as something solid, a sensation so all-pervading it was utterly crushing, and then the winch handle coming up again and the victim's hand reaching out to the galley where a knife lay, the fingers grasping for it.

I opened my eyes and a star streaked across the swaying hatch. I was on the floor, in a litter of galley equipment, and I had a knife in my hand. As I held it up, staring at it, dazed, the star streaked back across the hatch, the bottom of the mizzen sail showing suddenly white. The significance of that took a moment to sink in, so appalled was I by my experience. The star came and went again, the sail momentarily illuminated; then I was on my feet, clawing my way into the cockpit.

The sky was clear, studded with stars, and to the north the beam of Sumburgh Light swung clear. The fog had gone. There was a breeze from the east now. Somehow I managed to get the genoa hoisted, and inside of half an hour I was sailing in quiet waters clear of the roost.

I went below then and started clearing up the mess. The quarter berth was a tumbled pile of books from the shelf above, and as I was putting them back, a photograph fell to the floor. It showed a man and a woman and two children grouped round the wheel. The man was about 45, fair-haired with a fat, jolly face, his eyes squinting against bright sunlight. I have that picture still, my only contact with the man who had owned *Samoa* before me, the man whose ghostly presence haunted the ship.

By nightfall I was in Scalloway, tied up alongside a trawler at the pier. I didn't sell the boat. I couldn't afford to. And I didn't talk about it. Now that I had seen his picture, knew what he looked like, it seemed somehow less disturbing. I made up my mind I would have to live with it, whatever it was.

I never again used the quarter berth—in fact, I ripped it out of her before I left Scalloway. Sailing south I thought a lot about him in the long night watches. But though I speculated on what must have happened, and sometimes felt he was with me, I was never again identified with him.

Maybe I was never quite so tired again. But something I have to add. From the Azores I headed for Jamaica, and as soon as I arrived in Kingston the boat was the focus of considerable interest. She had apparently been stolen. At least, she had disappeared, and her owner with her. Hi-jacked was the word his solicitors used, for a merchant seaman named O'Sullivan, serving a six-year sentence for armed robbery, had escaped the night before and had never been heard of since. The police now believed he had boarded the boat, hi-jacked her and her owner and sailed her across the Atlantic, probably with Ireland as his objective.

I didn't attempt to see his wife. My experience—what I thought I now knew—could only add to her grief. I sailed at once for the Canal. But though I have tried to put it out of my mind, there are times when I feel his presence lingering. Maybe writing this will help. Maybe it will exorcise his poor, frightened ghost from my mind—or from the boat—whichever it is.

Hallowe'en for Mr Faulkner

AUGUST DERLETH

In America, ghosts have become traditionally so acknowledged that they have a special day of recognition each year, Hallowe'en, which falls on October 31st. Although the custom of celebrating this, the last night of summer, is Celtic in origin, it is only in America that it is still observed as something of a national festival, with children in particular taking part in harmless rituals such as the famous 'trick or treat' in which—suitably disguised as ghosts or witches—they threaten to scare neighbours unless they are given a small reward. The newspapers and television make a great point of the 'denizens of the dark' who are supposed to be abroad on this night which heralds the beginning of winter, and many a ghost story is told around blazing fires in rural districts. One great chronicler of rural America, and a macabre fiction writer into the bargain, was August Derleth, who described numerous strange occult experiences in his work. One such was a wraith-like figure which he saw one Hallowe'en. 'It was a very foggy night back in the Fifties,' he said, 'and I saw through a window a thin, caped figure dressed in what looked like Seventeenth-Century clothes. It disappeared almost immediately and I waited for ages for a knock at the door, expecting it to be a child about to 'trick or treat' me. Nothing happened, and the following day I learned that no children in the district had been allowed out that night because of the weather.' At this same time, Derleth had been reading a book about Guy Fawkes and the Plot to blow up the Houses of Parliament in November 1605. His mystery ghost looked as if it might just have been one of the plotters, he thought, and not wanting to waste a remarkable experience, sat down and wrote "Hallowe'en for Mr. Faulkner".

There was simply no use going farther; so Guy Faulkner stood where he was, as helpless as if he were in the midst of a chartless sea. He was somewhere in London, in a sea of fog? Was it in Lambeth? And had he not heard the bells of St Clement's? He deplored his insistence on going out that afternoon in trace of some faint lead to supplement the work being done by Inigo Gunter, who was an expert in matters historical and genealogical, and whose report had been promised him this very day. A pox on his own impatience! Now there was no telling just when he would escape the fog.

He stood resolutely still. Sooner or later someone was bound to come along. If it were a bobby, he would be given good conduct to his hotel. If it were anyone at all familar with the district, he might at least learn where he had wandered to. The fog swirled around him, growing ever more dense—not yellow, as he had been led to believe, but a kind of grey shot through with a glow rising as from distant lights which had no separate identity. He quelled his impatience; he had no alternative but to wait. He would have been almost as helpless in Chicago or New York, for all his familarity with those cities, so thick was the fog.

Quite suddenly a dark shape loomed beside him.

'Pardon me,' he said.

'Match, Guvnor?'

Faulkner took out his lighter. Fortunately, it lit at once. He held it up.

The fog played tricks on him. The face he looked into might have been his own. It bent to light a pipe, seemed to flatten, to dissolve—the fog again.

'I'm afraid I'm lost,' said Faulkner.

'Come along,' said the other, beginning to move away.

Faulkner followed. His companion walked with sureness and ease; he at least could find his way.

'I want to go to the Chelsea,' he said.

But the other did not reply, and Faulkner had all he could do to keep up with him, trying to keep from falling over kerbs and colliding with lamp-posts. Should there not have been more light as they approached the hotel? he wondered. But abruptly his silent companion turned off the walk and mounted a few steps. Faulkner was conscious of a typical iron railing at either side. Coming up behind his guide, Faulkner lit his lighter again; the figure 16 gleamed on the heavy door. Then the door swung open upon a darkened hall, and immediately his guide was engulfed. Faulkner hesitated only a moment—anything was better than the oppressive fog. The door closed behind him, and another opened before upon a dimly lit room into which he had hardly stepped before he was aware of the strangeness of it—a room, as it were, of invaluable antique furnishings; it might have been lifted completely from a museum. He turned to his companion to ask—and found himself alone.

The door behind him closed. Down along one wall of the room was another door, beneath which showed a brighter light; and behind it rose the murmur of voices. Had his companion gone that way? But no, how could he? There had not been time. A sudden panic assailed Faulkner and he turned to go back the way he had come.

But even as his hand fell upon the knob, the door at the end of the room opened, a yellow glow spread into the room, and a hearty voice said to someone behind, 'Here's Guy now! We were waiting for you.'

Faulkner turned, surprised. A man masked with a domino. And in costume. Behind him, grouped about a table, were others, likewise costumed and masked. But, of course, the night was near to All Hallows and some people celebrated the time of masks throughout the week, into November; these were doubtless traditional masks, and known to him, perhaps, behind their masks. He hesitated but a moment more; the man before him held the door invitingly open, and his smile bade Faulkner welcome as no words need have done.

'You're late, Guy . . .'

'We thought you'd failed of coming . . .'

'What kept you?'

A chair was pushed forward for him.

Bewildered, he sat down. He was aware of a strange kind of apprehension within him, as if something ominous lay behind this mask of comradeship. He could not remember a voice, a face, a gesture. And yet, so familiar were these men, that he could not but wonder how he could have forgotten them. In a moment, certainly, their names would come to him; someone would mention them.

'I say, Wright, now Guy's here, we can get on with it.'

Wright—John Wright, Faulkner said to himself. And that man talking was Tom Winter. And that, Robert Catesby. And the fourth, Tom Percy. And finally, Ambrose Rokewood. Faulkner could not recall where he had met them, yet their names were now certainly coming back to him. But the feeling of apprehension did not leave him.

He waited.

The bottles and glasses were pushed aside, and Catesby leaned over.

'The day's been chosen, you'll recollect, Guy.'

'The fifth,' said Winter.

One of them chuckled. 'Was it not a clever thing to have chosen a night of this week for our last meeting? When so many are in costume, and the most improbable of all excites no question?'

'But for your own, Guy,' said Wright. 'A strange costume, indeed. And unmasked! How bold!'

'Ah, I am but an humble servant of Mr Percy,' Faulkner said, and grinned.

But simultaneously he thought: Percy—but of course, he was employed by Percy. Had he not come over the sea from Flanders not long since? And spoken there with Stanley of Deventer? What nagged in his mind was a perplexity indeed. A broader ocean, a strange land, great cities . . .

'The powder's laid,' continued Catesby.

'Aye, and the fuse is placed,' said Percy. 'He had good time in which to do these things from my house next door to Parliament House. A good and willing servant, indeed. Once this business is done with, I commend him to you. He will go to heights.'

'One way or t'other,' said Wright sourly. 'High by his skill or by the scaffold if we're caught.'

'Come, come, let us not speak of being caught,' protested Catesby. 'We've come a long way; we are on the threshold of success. Victory will be ours within the week, mark me.'

'Who will light the fuse?' asked Rokewood. 'I offer myself.'

'Noble and generous Rokewood,' said Catesby. 'But this would scarce be fair to the others who are as eager to consummate this task. Shall we not draw for it?'

'Aye,' said Wright.

And 'Aye,' said Percy.

Winter nodded, without saying anything, and Rokewood made no protest.

'It will be arranged before this night is done. Come now, let us look to plans to which we must adhere once the thing has been accomplished. Draw closer.'

Catesby produced a map and spread it before them. Six heads circled it. Catesby's elegant fingers, dark against the white ruff at his wrist, descended to the map.

'The moment it is done, I will ride to my mother's house at Ashby St Legers. We shall, several of us, ride through Warwickshire to rally the country behind us. I myself will go straight to Digby and enlist his aid, by which time he will be ready, if I can tell him both James and Salisbury are dead.'

'And what if they are not?' asked Rokewood.

'We dare not fail.'

'There are thirty-six barrels of gunpowder under coal and faggots in the cellar. More than a ton of the stuff,' said Percy.

'But, since it's been there so long—May, was it not?— what assurance have we that it has not got wet?'

'It was put in a dry place on purpose,' said Percy, and turned to Faulkner. 'Was it not, Guy?'

Faulkner nodded.

'And the Jesuits?'

'We have Garnet's blessing, at least. But Greenway and Gerard know our plan and have not spoken against it.'

A doubt beset Faulkner. He closed his eyes. Instantly all this elaborate play was alien. He was Guy Faulkner of New York, in London in pursuing his genealogical studies. The year was 1953. But when he opened his eyes a moment later, he could have taken solemn oath that it was some other year. The candles flickered, and appurtenances of the house loomed grotesque in their age in the candlelight. The five masked men who stood about him, leaning over the map on the table, were impeccably dressed in the costumes of the seventeenth century's turn.

An elaborate hoax. Who could have been responsible for

it? Or, for that matter, for his own words, spoken so glibly? Or was it a plot, indeed? Was it by some accident that he had stumbled upon an attempt to repeat history, to blow up Parliament? Apprehension spread through him again.

'Guy says little,' said Wright suddenly.

'I am not man for words,' Faulkner responded without hesitation.

'True,' agreed Catesby. 'Would that all others had to his credit Guy's deeds. We should not now be in doubt of the success of our plot. Where is Tresham?'

'None knows. Safe in his bed, most likely,' said Percy.

'I said it was a mistake to invite Tresham to take part in this,' said Rokewood heavily. 'Monteagle is his brother-in-law; can he contrive to keep him from Parliament and destruction with James and Salisbury?'

'He dare not.'

'Who will say him nay? Was he not all eagerness and will at the beginning; but now that the thing is all but done, where is Tresham?' demanded Rokewood. 'A peer's brother-in-law has no place among us.'

'A man's a man not by any accident of blood,' said Catesby.

'Nor of religion, then,' said Percy.

'Agreed,' said Catesby. 'Or colour, age, or temper.'

All this time Winter had said nothing. Now he put on the table six sticks he had been fashioning. All save one were of equal length; the one was shorter.

'How say we?' he asked.

'He who draws the short stick shall light the fuse,' said Catesby.

There was an immediate chorus of agreement.

Catesby slipped on his gloves, so that he might not himself feel which was the short one among them, picked up the sticks, rolled them about a little, and held them out, stuck in his fist.

Percy drew first.

Then Rokewood. Since both had sticks of equal length, neither had drawn the short one.

Winter drew—a long stick.

Wright—another of similar length.

Catesby grinned sardonically, and held the two remaining sticks before Faulkner. 'It lies between us, Guy. Fate would have it so.'

Faulkner drew. He had the short stick.

Catesby opened his hand, let the remaining stick fall. 'I congratulate you, Guy. None could better perform this task to free our great country from the oppressions of James and Salisbury.'

Faulkner smiled. Uncertainty, apprehension, astonishment vied for revelation, but none showed on his features.

'You'll remember what was agreed upon,' Catesby went on. 'You'll get into the cellar in the night, and, as soon as the King has arrived, light the fuse and make your escape at once. Fly to join me at Ashby St Legers.'

Rokewood came to his feet, a heavy man, dark of feature. He reached behind him for his cloak. 'The thing's as good as done. I bid you goodnight, Gentlemen. May God attend our plans!'

One by one they withdrew, until only Catesby was left.

'You've not moved, Guy. Is anything wrong?'

'I must have time to think on this,' said Faulkner.

'Ten days, no more. The calendar marks the twenty-fifth of the month. In six more, November's upon us, and within the week beyond that James and Salisbury will be no more!' He stuck out his hand to shake Faulkner's. 'Good luck, Guy. We'll to victory or hang with you.' At the threshold he turned for a final word. 'I trust when again we meet at this place, 'twill be Old Paradise no longer, but New!'

Then he was gone.

Faulkner sat alone and for the moment, unmoving. How quixotic were his thoughts! Were it possible for a man to step back into time, he might have done so. The time would be 1605, the event the Gunpowder Plot against James I and Lord Salisbury. But in his mind was a core of turgid confusion. How was it possible for him to remember so well these people with whom he had sat this night and yet never met?

Was there, indeed, a hoax that intended him for victim? Or was there, on the other hand, a danger that there was indeed some plan afoot to blow up Parliament? He grew cold with fear. Something must be done to prevent such a plan's fulfillment. But what?

Who was it had mentioned Tresham and Lord Monteagle?

He looked wildly about him; there was not much time. At any moment he might be interrupted. The householder might come back. Wright, it seemed, was owner here. Or was it but another of Catesby's houses?

He came upon paper, a quill pen, ink.

'My lord, out of the love I bear to some of your friends, I have a care for preservation. Therefore I would advise you, as you tender your life, to devise some excuse to shift of your attendance of this Parliament, for God and man hath concurred to punish the wickedness of this time. And think not slightly of this advertisement, but retire yourself into your country, where you may expect the event in safety, for though there be no appearance of any stir, yet I say they shall receive a terrible blow, the Parliament, and yet they shall not see who hurts them. This counsel is not to be condemned, because it may do you good and can do you no harm, for the danger is past as soon as you have burnt the letter, and I hope God will give you the grace to make good use of it, to whose holy protection I commend you.'

Without hesitation, he signed it, 'Tresham'. His own name would have no meaning to Lord Monteagle. He folded the letter, folded another paper around it so devised to hold it as might an envelope, of which he saw none, wrote Lord Monteagle's name in a bold hand on the outside, and, without another glance for his surroundings, fled the room, fled the next, and in a few moments was outside and running through the fog as fast as possible, until he found a postman's box, and there dropped his letter, trusting that it would reach Monteagle in time. Ten days. He felt for his lighter, but he had left it, as he had his hat. He would not retrace his steps.

The air stirred him, the close-pressing fog brought him once again to awareness that he was lost. But no, not quite; was that not Westminster Bridge ahead? He walked on, and soon found himself above the Thames, with the fog beginning to thin.

Though it was past midnight, Gunter was still waiting for him. Not because he had intended to do so, but because he had fallen asleep in Faulkner's room. He started awake under Faulkner's touch.

'I've been asleep,' he said, ruefully, looking at his watch. 'And missed a nightcap with Barry.'

'Have one with me,' said Faulkner, moving towards the decanter. 'I've had an evening.'

'In this fog!'

'It's beginning to lift.' Faulkner came back with glasses and the decanter. 'What have you found?'

'Ah, something of interest, indeed,' said Gunter, becoming alert at once. 'Though I've no way of knowing how you'll take it.' He tossed off a drink and complimented Faulkner. 'It's all in these papers.' He took them out of his pocket, tapped them intimately where he held them in his hand, and gave them to Faulkner.

'I've got you back as far as York. The name was changed, you see, in 1605. Used to be Fawkes. Family of Edward Fawkes of York. It was Edward's son Guy . . .'

'The Gunpowder Plot!'

'Of course. The disgrace of it upon the family brought about the change in name. One understands that, of course. But no doubt you Americans look upon these things in a more romantic light.'

Faulkner's mouth went dry; his whisky was tasteless on his tongue.

He opened the papers and read of the succession of the line of Edward Fawkes, father of Guy Fawkes, who lent his name forever to the Gunpowder Plot to blow up Parliament with King James I and his ministers . . .

In the clear light of morning, he knew what he must do. He had a perfect excuse—to look for his hat and lighter. True, he did not know the address, but had not one of them spoken of 'Old Paradise', and was there not a street by that name not far from the Thames, off Westminster Bridge?

On that chance he called a cab. 'Take me to Old Paradise Street.'

There was no question. He got in, settled back, and was soon rolling towards his destination. The number, he remembered, was 16.

Someone had made game of him for Hallowe'en—which was odd, for not many of the British celebrated All Hallows. Who they were, Faulkner would soon know. There was no fog this morning to confuse him.

The cab rolled over Westminster Bridge and soon after came to a halt.

'Old Paradise, sir,' said the driver.

Faulkner got out, paid him and let him go. He walked slowly up the street. He could hardly hope to find any familiar facet, for the thick fog of the preceding evening had shrouded everything unrecognizably. Even the walk beneath his feet felt different. It had had the feel of cobbles in the night.

A short street. But there was no number 16.

He stood for a moment puzzled. But a postman coming along gave him hope and he stopped him.

'Number 16?' said the postman. 'I'm old enough to remember that. Before the war. It's rubble now. Come along, I'll show you where it was.'

Faulkner followed him, and they came presently to a cellar filled with rubble. There had once been a house there, and steps leading up to it, and iron railings about it. The railings were still there. Beyond, all was rubble. But not far from where they stood, in the rubble, lay the same numerals Faulkner had seen less than a day ago—not bright and gleaming now, but old, worn, bent. And beyond that . . .?'

'They've not got around to clean up here yet,' said the postman apologetically. 'The place was hit not long after Coventry. Historic house, too. Said to have been used as a meeting place for the Gunpowder plotters. Oh, I say now, you'd better not go climbing about in that rubble, sir—it's posted and dangerous.'

But Faulkner had gone ahead.

He felt he had the best right in the world to do so. Hoax, hallucination, dream—whatever had happened to him, he meant to retrieve his hat and the lighter which lay gleaming not far from it in the middle of the ruin and a little towards the rear—just where the room with the table would have been—if there had been such a room—and such a house. . . . New Paradise indeed!

He went back to his hotel and telephoned Inigo Gunter.

'Tell me, did they ever find out who wrote that letter to Lord Monteagle in the Gunpowder affair?'

'No, Mr Faulkner, to the best of my knowledge, they did not. They thought it was Tresham, but he denied it and died in the Tower. He might have won his freedom.'

'Never mind, Mr Gunter, I did it myself.'

That was a break he had not meant to make, he told himself after he had been cut off. He had meant to voice his belief that Guy Fawkes had written to Monteagle and disclosed the plot. But to call Gunter again and explain would only complicate matters more.

Inigo Gunter entertained his colleagues for weeks with his anecdote about the mad American and his delusion.

The Ghost

RICHARD HUGHES

*Among the many thousands of ghost stories—both wholly fictional and
those based on fact—there are not many that are written from the
spirit's point of view. No author—to my knowledge—has been on
the other side and returned to tell the tale, and therefore anything from
that standpoint is a real test of ingenuity and skill, The best story of
this kind which I know is the following short chiller by Richard
Hughes, indisputably one of today's greatest writers and the author
of that enduring classic, "A High Wind in Jamaica". Not so long
ago I was involved in the compilation of a book of Welsh fantasy
stories. Richard Hughes helped me and he told me then of several
encounters with the supernatural that he had had as a boy. He also
recalled the awful spectre which terrified him half to death when—as*

he put it—'I wandered, alone, under a waning moon, after midnight, with a sack of stolen peat on my back, near a prehistoric altar stone on the hillside.' In two or three other short stories he has explored the effects of people meeting spirits of the dead, but nowhere has he been more surprising than in "The Ghost"—and please don't spoil the effect of the ending by reading it first!

He killed me quite easily by crashing my head on the cobbles. *Bang!* Lord, what a fool I was! All my hate went out with that first bang: a fool to have kicked up that fuss just because I had found him with another woman. And now he was doing this to me—*bang!* That was the second one, and with it *everything* went out.

My sleek young soul must have glistened somewhat in the moonlight: for I saw him look up from the body in a fixed sort of way. That gave me an idea: I would haunt him. All my life I had been scared of ghosts: now I was one myself, I would get a bit of my own back. *He* never was: he said there weren't such things as ghosts. Oh, weren't there! I'd soon teach him. John stood up, still staring in front of him: I could see him plainly: gradually all my hate came back. I thrust my face close up against his: but he didn't seem to see it, he just stared. Then he began to walk forward, as if to walk through me: and I was afeard. Silly, for me—a spirit— to be afeard of his solid flesh: but there you are, fear doesn't act as you would expect, ever: and I gave back before him, then slipped aside to let him pass. Almost he was lost in the street-shadows before I recovered myself and followed him.

And yet I don't think he could have given me the slip: there was still something between us that drew me to him— willy-nilly, you might say, I followed him up to High Street, and down Lily Lane.

Lily Lane was all shadows: but yet I could still see him as clear as if it was daylight. Then my courage came back to me: I quickened my pace till I was ahead of him—turned round, flapping my hands and making a moaning sort of noise like the ghosts did I'd read of. He began to smile a little, in a sort of satisfied way: but yet he didn't seem properly to see me. Could it be that his hard disbelief in ghosts made him so that he *couldn't* see me? '*Hoo!*' I whistled through my small teeth. '*Hoo! Murderer! Murderer!*'—Someone flung up a top window. 'Who's that?' she called. 'What's the matter?'—So other people could hear, at any rate. But I kept silent: I wouldn't give him away—not yet. And all the time he walked straight forward, smiling to himself. He never had any conscience, I said to myself: here he is with new murder on his mind, smiling as easy as if it was nothing. But there was a sort of hard look about him, *all* the same.

It was odd, my being a ghost so suddenly when ten minutes ago I was a living woman and now, walking on air, with the wind clear and wet between my shoulder-blades. Ha-ha! I gave a regular shriek and a screech of laughter, it all felt so funny . . . surely John must have heard *that*: but no, he just turned the corner into Pole Street.

All along Pole Street the plane-trees were shedding their leaves: and then I knew what I would do. I made those dead leaves rise up on their thin edges, as if the wind was doing it. All along Pole Street they followed him, pattering on the roadway with their five dry fingers. But John just stirred among them with his feet, and went on: and I followed him: for as I said, there was still some tie between us that drew me.

Once only he turned and seemed to see me: there was a sort of recognition in his face: but no fear, only triumph. 'You're glad you've killed me,' thought I, 'but I'll make you sorry!'

And then all at once the fit left me. A nice sort of Christian, I, scarcely fifteen minutes dead and still thinking of revenge, instead of preparing to meet my Lord! Some sort of voice in me seemed to say: 'Leave him, Millie, leave him alone *before it is too late*!' Too late? Surely I could leave him when I wanted to? Ghosts haunt as they like, don't they? I'd make just one more attempt at terrifying him: then I'd give it up and think about going to Heaven.

He stopped, and turned, and faced me full.

I pointed at him with both my hands.

'John!' I cried. 'John! It's all very well for you to stand there, and smile, and stare with your great fish-eyes and think you've won: but you haven't! I'll do you. I'll *finish* you! I'll——'

I stopped, and laughed a little. Windows shot up. 'Who's that? What's the row?'—and so on. They had all heard: but he only turned and walked on.

'Leave him, Millie, before it is too late,' the voice said.

So that's what the voice meant: leave him before I betrayed his secret, and had the crime of revenge on my soul. Very well, I would: I'd leave him. I'd go straight to Heaven before any accident happened. So I stretched up my two arms, and tried to float into the air: but at once some force seized me like a great gust, and I was swept away after him down the street. There was something stirring in me that still bound me to him.

Strange, that I should be so real to all those people that they thought me still a living woman: but he—who had most reason to fear me, why, it seemed doubtful whether he even saw me. And where was he going to, right up the desolate long length of Pole Street?—He turned into Rope Street. I saw a blue lamp: that was the Police Station.

'Oh, Lord,' I thought, 'I've done it! Oh, Lord, he's going to give himself up!'

'You drove him to it,' the voice said. 'You fool, did you think he didn't see you? What did you expect? Did you think he's shriek, and gibber with fear at you? Did you think your John was a coward?—Now his death is on your head!'

'I didn't do it, I didn't!' I cried. 'I never wished him any harm, never, not *really*! I wouldn't hurt him, not for anything, I wouldn't. Oh, John, don't stare like that! There's still time . . . time!'

And all this while he stood in the door, looking at me, while the policemen came out and stood round him in a ring. He couldn't escape now.

'Oh, John,' I sobbed, 'forgive me! I didn't mean to do it! It was jealousy, John, what did it . . . because I loved you.'

Still the police took no notice of him.

'That's her,' said one of them in a husky voice. 'Done it with a hammer, she done it . . . brained him. But, Lord, isn't her face ghastly? Haunted, like.'

'Look at her 'ead, poor girl. Looks as if she tried to do herself in with the 'ammer, after.'

Then the sergeant stepped forward.

'Anything you say will be taken down as evidence against you.'

'John!' I cried softly, and held out my arms—for at last his face had softened.

'Holy Mary!' said one policeman, crossing himself. 'She's seeing him!'

'They'll not hang her,' another whispered. 'Did you notice her condition, poor girl?'

The Case of the Red-headed Women

DENNIS WHEATLEY

As I said in my introduction to the last story, no author has been on the 'other side' to report the ghost's point of view, but professional ghost hunters, spiritualists and others have devoted a great deal of time trying to establish the exact nature of these phenomena—as spirits surely are. Apart from seances at which mediums—men or women believed to be especially sensitive to the spirit world—try to communicate with the dead, there has been much experimentation with high speed cameras, sound recording equipment and machinery alert to all changes of atmospheric conditions, in an attempt to capture some kind of visible record. Our next story is about an inquiry of this kind, and few readers will need any introduction to its author, Dennis Wheatley, a very popular supernatural and historical novelist.

Although, as he has stressed on more than one occasion, Dennis Wheatley has no actual experience of Black Magic, Witchcraft and the other strange occult practices—believing that it is dangerous to meddle with such things—he has had a vivid brush with a ghost which he recalls clearly to this day. It happened when he was at school at Margate. He was climbing the stairs to his dormitory one night, he says, when he saw 'A white blob staring malevolently through the bannisters.' He goes on 'I screamed and ran downstairs and told the masters. They thought it might be a burglar and went looking for it with hockey sticks. But later I found out it was a ghost. The headmaster dabbled in spiritualism.' Many of his stories are the result of information sent to him by admirers, but "The Case of the Red-Headed Women" is unique in being partly based on a remarkable ghost hunter he knew personally, a flat in South Kensington that he visited and which no one would live in because of a succession of suicides that had occurred there, and . . . that childhood encounter on the stairs.

Neils Orsen waited, his long, tapering fingers beating a tattoo upon the mantelpiece, his large, curiously pale blue eyes thoughtful. There was no reason for his waiting, he had made no appointment, yet the moment the door opened and he saw the tall American lawyer from the Chambers below he knew that his instinct had not failed him—his friend was very worried.

'What's the trouble, Hemmingway?' he asked at once. 'Mix yourself a drink, then sit down and tell me all about it.'

The dark-haired solicitor gave the little man a shrewd smile as he helped himself to a whisky-and-soda. 'I suppose by now I should be used to this trick of yours of always knowing what's in my mind the moment I come into the room—or perhaps before—but it still seems queer. And of course you're right—I am worried—very worried.' He leant forward suddenly. 'Orsen, this is not an ordinary case—but I think it's right down your street.'

'Well?' his host smiled.

'The situation is this,' Hemmingway began. 'A young friend of mine has just got married. He has taken an apparently charming little flat and the lease was handled by my firm, but unfortunately I was away when the deal was drafted.'

'Unfortunately?' Orsen queried.

'Yes. It just happens that I know the history of the place and I wouldn't willingly have drafted a lease of it for my worst enemy. Of course outwardly it's an amazing bargain. Owing to the fact that it has been empty for so long the rental has been reduced out of all proportion to the value of the property.'

'Why?' Orsen interrupted encouragingly.

'Well, there have been three suicides and the other tenants have always left after a week or so, complaining of an unpleasantly cold atmosphere and all telling the same curious story that on certain nights the bathroom window used to open of its own accord.'

'Was there anything unusual about these suicides?'

'On the face of it, no,' Hemmingway continued slowly, drawing at his cigarette. 'The first was a French woman of about thirty; the second, which occurred some three months later, a man of sixty; and the third an older woman—who, incidentally, was the last occupant—she died just a year ago. Of course it may only be coincidence, but it seems very odd that all three should have chosen the bathroom window out of which to throw themselves.'

'Yes, most peculiar,' Orsen agreed, 'but there may be a perfectly reasonable explanation. As you know, four-fifths of the so-called psychic phenomena that I have to investigate turn out to be hoaxes, even though sometimes they are of a very violent and unpleasant nature. However, this may be one of the odd fifth, a genuine Saati manifestation; but what would you like me to do?'

'Just this. The flat is being re-decorated while the young couple are on their honeymoon and they will be returning in

about a month's time. I've got a set of keys, so I thought that
if you could go down there and see it maybe you'd know if
anything really is wrong. I, personally, am quite convinced
that there is something uncanny going on, and knowing your
peculiar power to sense psychic manifestations I came to
you. Anyway, the police would just laugh at me.'

Neils Orsen turned his head. 'Pãst! Pãst!' he called. As if
from nowhere a beautiful Siamese cat leapt down on to his
shoulder. 'Pãst, old man, we've been asked to go ghost-
hunting again. What do you think?'

The cat purred lazily and blinked its large, pale blue eyes
at Hemmingway.

Orsen held out his hand. 'Very well. Let me have the keys
and I'll see what I can do. Come back in a few days' time
and I'll give you the results.'

'Thanks awfully; that's a great load off my mind,'
Hemmingway said, finishing his drink. 'The flat is in
Collingburn Court, South Kensington; No. 35, and it's on
the fifth floor.'

A week later the two men met for dinner. Not until coffee
had been served would Orsen satisfy Hemmingway's
curiosity.

'In a way you were right,' he began. 'That place has a
most unpleasant atmosphere. I have been several times and
even spent the night there in the bathroom, but I found no
evidence of anything supernatural. The bad atmosphere is
easily explained. Many people who like myself are of
Nordic extraction are what you call *fey*, and as the seventh
child of a seventh child I am so ultra-sensitive that I can
pick up the unhappy vibrations of humans who have been
miserable at some time or another, in at least one out of
every six rooms I go into. Pãst didn't like it either. As you
know, I always take him with me on cases like this because
of his hyper-sensitiveness to evil manifestations.

'Being stymied in that direction I went to the police and
made inquiries about the suicides. The first was a very

beautiful French woman, Victorine Daubert, who lived alone with her maid. The maid was away when her suicide occurred. The second, curiously enough, was an inmate of the same block; a shipowner named Arnold Robertson. His flat was just above but he took over Madame Daubert's on her death owing to its greater accommodation. The last, Mrs Matheson, killed herself after a tenancy of only one week!

'Three points that did strike me as curious emerged from my inquiry; they are: one, that none of these people apparently had any motive for taking their lives; two, that all three suicides occurred between midnight and one in the morning; and three, the curious coincidence that both the women had very fine heads of red hair. But if there is an evil entity in that flat it does not respond to any of the usual tests for haunting; so there it is. I'm afraid there is nothing more I can do—for the present, anyway.'

'I see.' A worried frown creased Hemmingway's forehead. 'But what do you mean, "for the present"?'

'Just this. I checked up the dates upon which the tragedies took place—not the ordinary calendar dates but by the lunar months—and found that both the women committed suicide on the second day after the new moon. Of course this may mean nothing, because Mr Robertson threw himself out of the window on the fifteenth day, so there is no question of a series. But all the same, I think it would be worth my while to pay another visit two days after the next new moon. That is in about a fortnight's time and if there is any genuine Saati manifestation it should certainly take place that night. If not—well then, my dear Hemmingway, your young friends will have nothing to worry about. Oh, by the way, when do they return?'

'In about three weeks, I think.'

'Well, then, I suggest that we should both go down there a fortnight from today. What do you say?'

'That's grand by me. What time shall I meet you?' Hemmingway asked.

'It is no use our going there before midnight, so how about having a late dinner first? I will make all my arrangements that morning.'

'What do you mean, "arrangements"?'

'Oh, I shall place my special cameras in focus with the fatal window and connect up the flashlights with invisible wires. If the window is thrown open the flashlights will go off and should any psychic phenomenon appear the plates will be quite certain to register it upon their delicate surfaces.'

At eleven-thirty upon the pre-arranged evening Hemmingway and Orsen arrived at the block of flats.

As Orsen got out of the car he glanced up and gripping his companion by the arm whispered urgently: 'Look at those lights! Look! The bathroom is in darkness, but someone is in the bedroom.'

Hemmingway cursed. 'Burglars, I suppose.'

'We'll see,' Orsen replied grimly. Silently they climbed the stairs, then taking out his key he inserted it in the lock, but before he could turn it the door opened.

'Peter!' Hemmingway gasped. 'What on earth are you doing here? I thought——'

'I know. We weren't due back till next week and I was livid at having my honeymoon cut short but I was re-called on urgent business by my firm. As the flat was all ready we decided to come straight here from the station when the train got in tonight.'

The young man's tone was abrupt and he was obviously very tired, which perhaps accounted for the lack of surprise and pleasure he had shown upon seeing his friend.

It was an awkward situation. The last thing they wished to do was to ruin his first night in his new home by telling him of the true reason for their visit; so, having introduced Orsen, Hemmingway said quickly:

'I just thought I'd come round and see if everything was all right and as we were having dinner together I brought Orsen with me.'

Peter Wembley hesitated a moment; then his good manners overcame his reluctance to receiving visitors at such an hour after a long day of tiring travel. 'Well, it's grand to see you—come in, do. Pauline is getting ready for bed, but I was just going to have a night-cap, so you must join me.'

Hemmingway and Orsen filed past him, feeling acutely embarrassed. Their young host was obviously not very pleased to see them. Only by appearing boorish and insensitive could they keep him up for long and it was still a good twenty minutes before midnight.

'What will you have?' Peter went over to the sideboard. 'Whisky-and-soda—brandy or——'

'Whisky for me, old man,' Hemmingway said with a brightness he did not feel.

'And for you, sir?' Peter glanced at Orsen.

'May I have a glass of water? I find that it suits me best.'

The two guests sat down, but Peter stood in front of the fire rocking gently on his heels. He evidently had no intention of allowing them to prolong their visit into a midnight session.

Hemmingway glanced uneasily at Orsen, but the little man was saying with a guileless smile: 'I hear you've just returned from your honeymoon—do tell me, where did you go?'

'Italy—the south—little place called Amalfi—perhaps you know it?'

'Yes, I drove over to it once from Naples—an enchanting spot.'

Peter nodded, but he made no further contribution to the conversation.

'Of course you had good weather?' Orsen went on a little lamely.

'Um . . . too cold for bathing, but the blue skies were a pleasant change.'

For lack of something to say Orsen pulled out his cigarette-case. 'Will you have one of these? They are Turks, I have them specially imported for me.'

'No thanks.' Peter shook his head.

Hemmingway felt it was time that he entered the uneven contest. They'd only been there for just over ten minutes and somehow Peter had to be kept talking until well after midnight. 'By the way, old man,' he began jovially, 'I suppose you'll be doing some hunting now you're back.'

'Rather,' the young man showed more interest now that his favourite subject had been breached. 'I hope to get down to Leicestershire next week-end.'

'Have you still got that grand little mare you had last season?'

'Yes. She's stabled with some friends of mine; you must try her out one day.'

'Pauline's keen, too, isn't she?'

The mention of Peter's wife was unfortunate; he glanced pointedly towards the bedroom door. 'Yes. She'll be so sorry to have missed you, but I expect she's in bed by this time.'

The situation was becoming desperate. Suddenly the clock began to strike. The tiny chimes seemed to resound through the still room. Hemmingway looked up sharply, but Orsen shook his head, 'Fast,' his lips mouthed the word silently.

'I say, Peter.' Hemmingway leant forward quickly to attract his host's wandering attention, 'I had the most amusing case the other day. A young man came to me almost biting his nails with rage.'

'Really.' Peter tried to show some interest.

'Yes, it seems that his old man had done the dirty on him—left all his money to his mistress.'

'But surely he must have known what kind of man his father was and expected something like that to happen?' Orsen interrupted helpfully.

'No, no, that's the funny part, the old boy fooled him into thinking that he led a respectable and even puritanical life—pretended to disapprove heartily of modern young things—and his only ostensible form of fun was stamp collecting.'

'What was the girl like?'

'As tough as they make 'em. An innocent little thing you'd say, till she started to talk—you know the type, great big blue eyes and a mass of fluffy yellow hair. I think she was a chorus girl until old Standish picked her up,' Hemmingway trailed off lamely.

'Sickening for the boy,' Peter smothered a yawn.

Orsen began to tap his long tapering fingers on the table beside him. How much longer would they have to endure this wretched pretence of a casual visit; it was well past twelve now but nothing might happen for half an hour or more.

Hemmingway nerved himself to cross the room and refill his glass under Peter's openly disapproving stare. His thoughts were chaotic. Even while they sat there some terrible thing might be mounting unseen from the bottomless pit to claim another victim beyond the sitting-room walls.

'I believe stamp collecting is a very interesting pastime— have you ever gone in for it? A friend of mine . . .' Orsen began trying desperately to keep things going.

'No, I haven't.' Peter's voice was sharp and almost rude, and shrugging irritably he began to pace the room.

The two intruders sat on—miserably racking their brains for another subject. But Orsen found it impossible to concentrate. What was the girl doing; she should be in bed by now; she would be quite safe there—but was she in bed? Or had she still to go into the bathroom to wash? He listened intently. Only the ticking of the clock on the mantelpiece disturbed the eerie silence. They seemed to have been sitting there for hours.

Even Peter was affected by the strange tension that crept into the atmosphere. He slumped into a chair and stared at the floor, apparently no longer caring whether his guests went or not. Hemmingway smoked incessantly. The uncanny stillness enveloped them all like a mantle of fog. Only the clock ticked on the mantelpiece in mechanical defiance.

Orsen stirred uneasily; his sixth sense warned him that the moment of crisis was fast approaching. Suddenly he leapt to his feet and dashed towards the further door.

Peter came to earth with a jerk. 'Hi—where are you going? That's my wife's room!' he shouted angrily.

A piercing scream made them gasp as Orsen and Peter met and struggled in the doorway. Hemmingway grabbed Peter by the shoulder and hauled him back. Orsen dashed through the bedroom and was the first to reach the bathroom. It was in darkness; the window was flung wide open and a girl lay stretched on the floor beneath it. Peter, having flung Hemmingway off, leapt to the light switch but Orsen stopped him while Hemmingway picked the girl up and carried her into the bedroom.

While Peter was getting some brandy Orsen set about retrieving the cameras he had placed in the bathroom that morning. One that he had set at an angle on the top of the linen-cupboard was safe; but the other, which he had fixed up on a bracket just outside the window, was gone.

When he went in to Pauline's room she was recovering. Her large grey eyes were open and terrified and her bright auburn hair glittered under the sharp bedside light.

'What happened, darling? What happened?' Peter cried, his face pale and distraught.

She passed a hand over her forehead. 'I—I can't remember anything except that when I—before I got into bed I had the most appalling thirst. I went in to the bathroom to fetch a glass of water. It seemed frightfully hot in there so I opened the window, then'—she hesitated and shuddered—'a cold wind of incredible force seemed to sweep me up from behind and for a second I thought it was going to throw me bodily out of the window. A brilliant light flashed in my face —I remember screaming—then, I suppose, I fainted.'

Directly he could catch Hemmingway's eye, Orsen said

gently: 'Well, I think we had better be going. You'll be all right now, I promise you. We'll find our own way out—don't you bother, Mr Wembley.'

As he had visited the flats in the daytime Orsen knew that the one below had a balcony and fortunately the flat was temporarily unoccupied. Having dug out the porter of the block with his pass keys, they found Orsen's camera which by great good luck was not smashed to pieces, but had got lodged in the branches of a small bay tree.

Immediately they got back to Orsen's chambers in the Temple they set about developing the plates.

'Here's the first!' the frail little man announced excitedly. 'This is the one from the camera that was on the linen-cupboard.'

Hemmingway peered over his shoulder, but it was disappointing. It showed an outflung arm with fingers crooked clutching wildly at the empty air and a shadow just behind it that might have been almost anything.

'No, no good; but the second should be ready now, we'll see if that is any better,' Orsen said, hopefully. He turned after a moment. 'Yes—just look at this!'

Hemmingway stared at the plate. He saw Pauline Wembley's face, ghastly and terrified, her eyes black and fixed, her body foreshortened as though she was being hurled through the air; but over her shoulder there was another face, only imperfectly materialised, as through it could be seen the open door of the linen-cupboard.

'That's what I wanted,' Orsen breathed, and bent down to stroke Pāst, his Siamese cat, who was gently rubbing himself against his legs. Abruptly he straightened up. 'You must get your young friends out of that flat some time to-morrow on one pretext or other—anything will do—then we can go down there and deal with this horrible business thoroughly.'

'All right; I think I can manage that. Have you found an explanation?'

'Yes—I believe so.' Orsen suddenly seemed very tired and Hemmingway knew that the crisis in each of his investigations always told heavily on his frail physique, so he was not surprised when the little man added: 'But I'm too tired and done up to talk now. Call for me here tomorrow at whatever time is convenient and I'll tell you my conclusions.'

The next morning on their way down to South Kensington, Orsen explained. 'Evil entities of this kind,' he began, 'must have something to fasten on in order to aid their materialisation and make them physically dangerous. I guessed, the moment I saw Pauline Wembley's lovely red hair. All red-headed people give out a definite and curious emanation. In civilised countries this is rendered unnoticeable by extreme cleanliness—but it still remains apparent to astral sensitives. Now, as you know, apart from the suicides, three other women lived in the flat—uneasily, I grant you, but they came to no harm, as also the two men; but both the women who were supposed to have committed suicide—and Pauline Wembley who was attacked—had this peculiarity.'

'That's all very well, but how do you account for Robertson—his hair was black?' Hemmingway asked a trifle impatiently.

'If my theory is correct I shall be able to account for that when we arrive.'

On entering the flat they went straight into the bathroom. 'Look at the door of this linen-cupboard,' Orsen said. 'It is firmly shut and I am prepared to swear that it was shut last night when we rushed in here; yet in the photograph it is standing wide open. I'm convinced that this cupboard holds the key to the mystery,' and opening the door he began to remove the shelves.

'I rather think this cupboard has a false back,' he murmured a moment later. 'Yes, I was right. Look!'

Hemmingway peered inside as Orsen pulled forwards a

hinged sheet of three-ply that formed a second door. Behind it a small dark stairway led up towards the flat above.

'This is the way the Thing comes,' Orsen continued softly, 'and in this case we have to deal not with an Ab-human, but with an earth-bound. Now that we've found the root of the evil we can exorcise it. I will perform a ritual purification and the poor soul will be released from the chains that still bind it to the physical. Its time is up or the Great Ones who adjust the balances in the lives of us all would never have sent me here. Afterwards, your young friends will have nothing more to fear.'

'But—' Hemmingway broke in—'I still don't see how everything ties up. I understand what you said about only the emanations from red hair giving the Thing power to materialise physically and that being the reason why the other women were not attacked, but that does not explain the death of old Robertson.'

Orsen smiled. 'My friend, haven't you realised that the first woman, Victorine Daubert, didn't commit suicide at all? This stairway between the two flats is the key to the whole business. She was Robertson's mistress. He was jealous perhaps—in any case, he came down these stairs one night, caught her in the bathroom and murdered her by throwing her out of the window. Then, her personality preying on his mind, he took over the flat himself, lived there in misery for three months and eventually committed suicide by the same means as those by which he had killed her.'

'Two such occurrences are quite sufficient to explain his haunting the scenes of these terrible moments at certain phases of the moon. He has become a blind, seeking force which no longer recognises persons in this life and is compelled to repeat his murderous act whenever he has an opportunity.

'Each time he suffers all the agony of remorse he felt after the murder of Victorine Daubert until he can find a new victim; yet only the emanations of red hair give him the power to do so, then the wheel of his terrible penance starts to turn again.'

'It sounds extremely plausible, but how can you be certain?' Hemmingway asked with all a legal man's reluctance to admit anything but cold hard facts.

'Compare these two photographs,' Orsen held them out. 'The first which I got from Scotland Yard is of Robertson after he committed suicide. The second is the one of Pauline being thrown towards the window last night. Behind her you will see the outlines of a face which is quite sufficiently materialised to be recognised as Robertson's.'

'By Jove, you're right! But what prevented her from being hurled to her death?'

'The flashlight of my camera going off as the window opened and operated the leads I had fixed. The Powers of Darkness can always be driven back by the Powers of Light.'

Smoke Ghost

FRITZ LEIBER

Inquiry into the nature of ghosts has been going on with equal dedication here and in America, and some astonishing reports have been circulated in recent years, not to mention photographs which are actually claimed to be those of spirits. New theories have naturally enough resulted from this work, and several writers of fiction have taken these as the basis for highly unusual and entertaining stories. One such man is Fritz Leiber, a leading Science Fiction writer, who has been particularly intrigued by the idea that the traditional ghosts of the past are being superseded by a new breed of phantoms because of our rapidly changing life-styles. As he has written: 'The supernatural beings of a modern city would be quite different from the ghosts of yesterday. The Middle Ages built cathedrals and soon there were little grey shapes gliding around at night. Today, we deny all the old haunts and superstitions of cottages and castles. But instead we have created a new culture of sky-scrapers and apartment blocks and they are spawning a whole host of new demons.' Fritz Leiber had a ghost in his own past on which to draw for experience—although the encounter was rather more prosaic than his theory: as a young man he had toured America for a time as an actor, and in an old Mid-West theatre he had seen the ghost of a long dead actor prowling the wings. Nonetheless, you will find there is something of both the traditional and the ultra-modern in "Smoke Ghost".

Miss Millick wondered just what had happened to Mr Wran. He kept making the strangest remarks when she took dictation. Just this morning he had quickly turned around and asked, 'Have you ever seen a ghost, Miss Millick?' And she had tittered nervously and replied, 'When I was a girl there was a thing in white that used to come out of the closet in the attic bedroom when I slept there, and moan. Of course it was just my imagination. I was frightened of lots of things.' And he had said, 'I don't mean that kind of ghost. I mean a ghost from the world today, with the soot of the factories on its face and the pounding of machinery in its soul. The kind that would haunt coal yards and slip around at night through deserted office buildings like this one. A real ghost. Not something out of books.' And she hadn't known what to say.

He'd never been like this before. Of course he might be joking, but it didn't sound that way. Vaguely Miss Millick wondered whether he mightn't be seeking some sort of sympathy from her. Of course, Mr Wran was married and had a little child, but that didn't prevent her from having daydreams. The daydreams were not very exciting, still they helped fill up her mind. But now he was asking her another of those unprecedented questions.

'Have you ever thought what a ghost of our times would look like, Miss Millick? Just picture it. A smoky composite face with the hungry anxiety of the unemployed, the neurotic restlessness of the person without purpose, the jerky tension of the high-pressure metropolitan worker, the uneasy resentment of the striker, the callous opportunism of the scab, the aggressive whine of the panhandler, the inhibited terror of the bombed civilian, and a thousand other twisted emotional patterns. Each one overlying and yet blending with the other, like a pile of semitransparent masks?'

Miss Millick gave a little self-conscious shiver and said, 'That would be terrible. What an awful thing to think of.'

She peered furtively across the desk. She remembered having heard that there had been something impressively abnormal about Mr Wran's childhood, but she couldn't recall what it was. If only she could do something—laugh at his mood or ask him what was really wrong. She shifted the extra pencils in her left hand and mechanically traced over some of the shorthand curlicues in her notebook.

'Yet, that's just what such a ghost or vitalised projection would look like, Miss Millick,' he continued, smiling in a tight way. 'It would grow out of the real world. It would reflect the tangled, sordid, vicious things. All the loose ends. And it would be very grimy. I don't think it would seem white or wispy, or favour graveyards. It wouldn't moan. But it would mutter unintelligibly, and twitch at your sleeve. Like a sick, surly ape. What would such a thing want from a person, Miss Millick? Sacrifice? Worship? Or just fear? What could you do to stop it from troubling you?'

Miss Millick giggled nervously. There was an expression beyond her powers of definition in Mr Wran's ordinary, flat-cheeked, thirtyish face, silhouetted against the dusty window. He turned away and stared out into the grey downtown atmosphere that rolled in from the railroad yards and the mills. When he spoke again his voice sounded far away.

'Of course, being immaterial, it couldn't hurt you physically—at first. You'd have to be peculiarly sensitive to see it, or be aware of it at all. But it would begin to influence your actions. Make you do this. Stop you from doing that. Although only a projection, it would gradually get its hooks into the world of things as they are. Might even get control of suitably vacuous minds. Then it could hurt whomever it wanted.'

Miss Millick squirmed and read back her shorthand, like the books said you should do when there was a pause. She became aware of the failing light and wished Mr Wran would ask her to turn on the overhead. She felt scratchy, as if soot were sifting down on to her skin.

'It's a rotten world, Miss Millick,' said Mr Wran, talking at the window. 'Fit for another morbid growth of superstition. It's time the ghosts, or whatever you call them, took over and began a ride of fear. They'd be no worse than men.'

'But'—Miss Millick's diaphragm jerked, making her titter inanely—'of course, there aren't any such things as ghosts.'

Mr Wran turned around.

'Of course there aren't, Miss Millick,' he said in a loud, patronising voice, as if she had been doing the talking rather than he. 'Science and common sense and psychiatry all go to prove it.'

She hung her head and might even have blushed if she hadn't felt so all at sea. Her leg muscles twitched, making her stand up, although she hadn't intended to. She aimlessly rubbed her hand along the edge of the desk.

'Why, Mr Wran, look what I got off your desk,' she said, showing him a heavy smudge. There was a note of clumsily playful reproof in her voice. 'No wonder the copy I bring you always gets so black. Somebody ought to talk to those scrubwomen. They're skimping on your room.'

She wished he would make some normal joking reply. But instead he drew back and his face hardened.

'Well, to get back,' he rapped out harshly, and began to dictate.

When she was gone, he jumped up, dabbed his finger

experimentally at the smudged part of the desk, frowned worriedly at the almost inky smears. He jerked open a drawer, snatched out a rag, hastily swabbed off the desk, crumpled the rag into a ball and tossed it back. There were three or four other rags in the drawer, each impregnated with soot.

Then he went over to the window and peered out anxiously through the dusk, his eyes searching the panorama of roofs, fixing on each chimney and water tank.

'It's a neurosis. Must be. Compulsions. Hallucinations,' he muttered to himself in a tired, distraught voice that would have made Miss Millick gasp. 'It's that damned mental abnormality cropping up in a new form. Can't be any other explanation. But it's so damned real. Even the soot. Good thing I'm seeing the psychiatrist. I don't think I could force myself to get on the elevated tonight.' His voice trailed off, he rubbed his eyes, and his memory automatically started to grind.

It had all begun on the elevated. There was a particular little sea of roofs he had grown into the habit of glancing at just as the packed car carrying him homeward lurched around a turn. A dingy, melancholy little world of tar-paper, tarred gravel and smoky brick. Rusty tin chimneys with odd conical hats suggested abandoned listening posts. There was a washed-out advertisement of some ancient patent medicine on the nearest wall. Superficially it was like ten thousand other drab city roofs. But he always saw it around dusk, either in the smoky half-light, or tinged with red by the flat rays of a dirty sunset, or covered by ghostly wind-blown white sheets of rain-splash, or patched with blackish snow; and it seemed unusually bleak and suggestive; almost beautifully ugly though in no sense picturesque; dreary, but meaningful. Unconsciously it came to symbolise for Catesby Wran certain disagreeable aspects of the frustrated, frightened century in which he lived, the jangled century of hate and heavy industry and total wars. The quick daily glance into the half darkness became an integral part of his life. Oddly, he never saw it in the morning, for it was then his habit to sit on the other side of the car, his head buried in the paper.

One evening towards winter he noticed what seemed to be a shapeless black sack lying on the third roof from the tracks. He did not think about it. It merely registered as an addition to the well-known scene and his memory stored away the impression for further reference. Next evening, however, he decided he had been mistaken in one detail. The object was a roof nearer than he had thought. Its colour and texture, and the grimy stains around it, suggested that it was filled with coal dust, which was hardly reasonable. Then, too, the following evening it seemed to have been blown against a rusty ventilator by the wind—which could hardly have happened if it were at all heavy. Perhaps it was filled with leaves. Catesby was surprised to find himself anticipating his next daily glance with a minor note of apprehension. There was something unwholesome in the posture of the thing that stuck in his mind—a bulge in the sacking that suggested a misshaped head peering around the ventilator. And his apprehension was justified, for that evening the thing was on the nearest roof, though on the farther side, looking as if it had just flopped down over the low brick parapet.

Next evening the sack was gone. Catesby was annoyed at the momentary feeling of relief that went through him, because the whole matter seemed too unimportant to warrant feelings of any sort. What difference did it make if his imagination had played tricks on him, and he'd fancied that the object was slowly crawling and hitching itself closer across the roofs? That was the way any normal imagination worked. He deliberately chose to disregard the fact that there were reasons for thinking his imagination was by no means a normal one. As he walked home from the elevated, however, he found himself wondering whether the sack was really gone. He seemed to recall a vague, smudgy trail leading across the gravel to the nearer side of the roof, which was masked by a parapet. For an instant an unpleasant picture formed in his mind—that of an inky, humped creature crouched behind the parapet, waiting.

The next time he felt the familiar grating lurch of the car, he caught himself trying not to look out. That angered him. He turned his head quickly. When he turned it back, his compact face was definitely pale. There had been only time for a fleeting rearward glance at the escaping roof. Had he actually seen in silhouette the upper part of a head of some sort peering over the parapet? Nonsense, he told himself. And even if he had seen something, there were a thousand explanations which did not involve the supernatural or even true hallucination. Tomorrow he would take a good look and clear up the whole matter. If necessary, he would visit the roof personally, though he hardly knew where to find it and disliked in any case the idea of pampering a silly fear.

He did not relish the walk home from the elevated that evening, and visions of the thing disturbed his dreams, and were in and out of his mind all next day at the office. It was then that he first began to relieve his nerves by making jokingly serious remarks about the supernatural to Miss Millick, who seemed properly mystified. It was on the same day, too, that he became aware of a growing antipathy to grime and soot. Everything he touched seemed gritty, and he found himself mopping and wiping at his desk like an old lady with a morbid fear of germs. He reasoned that there was no real change in his office, and that he'd just now become sensitive to the dirt that had always been there, but there was no denying an increasing nervousness. Long before the car reached the curve, he was straining his eyes through the murky twilight, determined to take in every detail.

Afterwards he realised he must have given a muffled cry of some sort, for the man beside him looked at him curiously, and the woman ahead gave him an unfavourable stare.

Conscious of his own pallor and uncontrollable trembling, he stared back at them hungrily, trying to regain the feeling of security he had completely lost. They were the usual reassuringly wooden-faced people everyone rides home with on the elevated. But suppose he had pointed out to one of them what he had seen—that sodden, distorted face of sacking and coal dust, that boneless paw which waved back and forth, unmistakably in his direction, as if reminding him of a future appointment—he involuntarily shut his eyes tight. His thoughts were racing ahead to tomorrow evening. He pictured this same windowed oblong of light and packed humanity surging around the curve—then an opaque monstrous form leaping out from the roof in a parabolic swoop—an unmentionable face pressed close against the window, smearing it with wet coal dust—huge paws fumbling sloppily at the glass—

Somehow he managed to turn off his wife's anxious inquiries. Next morning he reached a decision and made an appointment for that evening with a psychiatrist a friend had told him about. It cost him a considerable effort, for Catesby had a well-grounded distaste for anything dealing with psychological abnormality. Visiting a psychiatrist meant raking up an episode in his past which he had never fully described even to his wife. Once he had made the decision, however, he felt considerably relieved. The psychiatrist, he told himself, would clear everything up. He could almost fancy him saying, 'Merely a bad case of nerves. However, you must consult the oculist whose name I'm writing down for you, and you must take two of these pills in water every four hours,' and so on. It was almost comforting, and made the coming revelation he would have to make seem less painful.

But as the smoky dusk rolled in, his nervousness had returned and he had let his joking mystification of Miss Millick run away with him until he had realised he wasn't frightening anyone but himself.

He would have to keep his imagination under better control, he told himself, as he continued to peer out restlessly at the massive, murky shapes of the downtown office buildings. Why, he had spent the whole afternoon building up a kind of neo-medieval cosmology of superstition. It wouldn't do. He realised then that he had been standing at the window much longer than he'd thought, for the glass panel in the door was dark and there was no noise coming from the outer office. Miss Millick and the rest must have gone home.

It was then he made the discovery that there would have been no special reason for dreading the swing around the curve that night. It was, as it happened, a horrible discovery. For, on the shadowed roof across the street and four stories below, he saw the thing huddle and roll across the gravel and, after one upward look of recognition, merge into the blackness beneath the water tank.

As he hurriedly collected his things and made for the elevator, fighting the panicky impulse to run, he began to think of hallucination and mild psychosis as very desirable conditions. For better or for worse, he pinned all his hopes on the psychiatrist.

'So you find yourself growing nervous and . . . er . . . jumpy, as you put it,' said Dr Trevethick, smiling with dignified geniality. 'Do you notice any more definite physical symptoms? Pain? Headache? Indigestion?'

Catesby shook his head and wet his lips. 'I'm especially nervous while riding in the elevated,' he murmured swiftly.

'I see. We'll discuss that more fully. But I'd like you first to tell me about something you mentioned earlier. You said there was something about your childhood that might predispose you to nervous ailments. As you know, the early years are critical ones in the development of an individual's behaviour pattern.'

Catesby studied the yellow reflections of frosted gloves in the dark surface of the desk. The palm of his left hand aimlessly rubbed the thick nap of the armchair. After a while he raised his head and looked straight into the doctor's small brown eyes.

'From perhaps my third to my ninth year,' he began, choosing the words with care, 'I was what you might call a sensory prodigy.'

The doctor's expression did not change. 'Yes?' he inquired politely.

'What I mean is that I was supposed to be able to see through walls, read letters through envelopes and books through their covers, fence and play ping-pong blindfolded, find things that were buried, read thoughts.' The words tumbled out.

'And could you?' The doctor's voice was toneless.

'I don't know. I don't suppose so,' answered Catesby, long-lost emotions flooding back into his voice. 'It's all confused now. I thought I could, but then they were always encouraging me. My mother . . . was . . . well . . . interested in psychic phenomena. I was . . . exhibited. I seem to remember seeing things other people couldn't. As if most opaque objects were transparent. But I was very young. I didn't have any scientific criteria for judgment.'

He was reliving it now. The darkened rooms. The earnest assemblages of gawking, prying adults. Himself alone on a little platform, lost in a straight-backed wooden chair. The black silk handkerchief over his eyes. His mother's coaxing, insistent questions. The whispers. The gasps. His own hate of the whole business, mixed with hunger for the adulation of adults. Then the scientists from the university, the experiments, the big test. The reality of those memories engulfed him and momentarily made him forget the reason why he was disclosing them to a stranger.

'Do I understand that your mother tried to make use of you as a medium for communicating with the . . . er . . . other world?'

Catesby nodded eagerly.

'She tried to, but she couldn't. When it came to getting in touch with the dead, I was a complete failure. All I could do —or thought I could do—was see real, existing three-dimensional objects beyond the vision of normal people. Objects anyone could have seen except for distance, obstruction, or darkness. It was always a disappointment to Mother.'

He could hear her sweetish, patient voice saying, 'Try again, dear, just this once. Katie was your aunt. She loved you. Try to hear what she's saying.' And he had answered, 'I can see a woman in a blue dress standing on the other side of Dick's house.' And she had replied, 'Yes, I know, dear. But that's not Katie. Katie's a spirit. Try again. Just this once, dear.' The doctor's voice gently jarred him back into the softly gleaming office.

'You mentioned scientific criteria for judgment, Mr Wran. As far as you know, did anyone ever try to apply them to you?'

Catesby's nod was emphatic.

'They did. When I was eight, two young psychologists from the university got interested in me. I guess they did it for a joke at first, and I remember being very determined to show them I amounted to something. Even now I seem to recall how the note of polite superiority and amused sarcasm drained out of their voices. I suppose they decided at first that it was very clever trickery, but somehow they persuaded Mother to let them try me out under controlled conditions. There were lots of tests that seemed very businesslike after Mother's slipshod little exhibitions. They found I was clairvoyant—or so they thought. I got worked up and on edge. They were going to demonstrate my supernormal sensory powers to the university psychology faculty. For the first time I began to worry about whether I'd come through. Perhaps they kept me going at too hard a pace, I don't know. At any rate, when the test came, I couldn't do a thing. Everything became opaque. I got desperate and made things up out of my imagination. I lied. In the end I failed utterly, and I believe the two young psychologists got into a lot of hot water as a result.'

He could hear the brusque, bearded man saying, 'You've been taken in by a child, Flaxman, a mere child. I'm greatly disturbed. You've put yourself on the same plane as common charlatans. Gentlemen, I ask you to banish from your minds this whole sorry episode. It must never be referred to.' He winced at the recollection of his feeling of guilt. But at the same time he was beginning to feel exhilarated and almost light-hearted. Unburdening his long-repressed memories had altered his whole viewpoint. The episodes on the elevated began to take on what seemed their proper proportions as merely the bizarre workings of overwrought nerves and an overly suggestible mind. The doctor, he anticipated confidently, would disentangle the obscure subconscious causes, whatever they might be. And the whole business would be finished off quickly, just as his childhood experience —which was beginning to seem a little ridiculous now—had been finished off.

'From that day on,' he continued, 'I never exhibited a trace of my supposed powers. My mother was frantic and tried to sue the university. I had something like a nervous breakdown. Then the divorce was granted, and my father got custody of me. He did his best to make me forget it. We went on long outdoor vacations and did a lot of athletics, associated with normal matter-of-fact people. I went to business college eventually, I'm in advertising now. But,' Catesby paused, 'now that I'm having nervous symptoms, I've wondered if there mightn't be a connection. It's not a question of whether I was really clairvoyant or not. Very likely my mother taught me a lot of unconscious deceptions, good enough to fool even young psychology instructors. But don't you think it may have some important bearing on my present condition?'

For several moments the doctor regarded him with a

professional frown. Then he said quietly, 'And is there some
. . . er . . . more specific connection between your experiences then and now? Do you by any chance find that you
are once again beginning to . . . er . . . see things?'

Catesby swallowed. He had felt an increasing eagerness to
unburden himself of his fears, but it was not easy to make a
beginning, and the doctor's shrewd question rattled him.
He forced himself to concentrate. The thing he thought he
had seen on the roof loomed up before his inner eye with
unexpected vividness. Yet it did not frighten him. He
groped for words.

Then he saw that the doctor was not looking at him but
over his shoulder. Colour was draining out of the doctor's
face and his eyes did not seem so small. Then the doctor
sprang to his feet, walked past Catesby, threw up the window
and peered into the darkness.

As Catesby rose, the doctor slammed down the window
and said in a voice whose smoothness was marred by a
slight, persistent gasping, 'I hope I haven't alarmed you.
I saw the face of . . . er . . . a Negro prowler on the fire
escape. I must have frightened him, for he seems to have
gotten out of sight in a hurry. Don't give it another thought.
Doctors are frequently bothered by *voyeurs* . . . er . . . Peeping
Toms.'

'A Negro?' asked Catesby, moistening his lips.

The doctor laughed nervously. 'I imagine so, though my
first odd impression was that it was a white man in blackface.
You see, the colour didn't seem to have any brown in it. It
was dead-black.'

Catesby moved towards the window. There were smudges
on the glass. 'It's quite all right, Mr Wran.' The doctor's
voice had acquired a sharp note of impatience, as if he
were trying hard to reassume his professional authority.
'Let's continue our conversation. I was asking you if you
were'—he made a face—'seeing things.'

Catesby's whirling thoughts slowed down and locked into

place. 'No, I'm not seeing anything that other people don't see, too. And I think I'd better go now. I've been keeping you too long.' He disregarded the doctor's half-hearted gesture of denial. 'I'll phone you about the physical examination. In a way you've already taken a big load off my mind.' He smiled woodenly. 'Good night, Dr Trevethick.'

Catesby Wran's mental state was a peculiar one. His eyes searched every angular shadow, he glanced sideways down each chasm-like alley and barren basement passageway, and kept stealing looks at the irregular line of the roofs, yet he was hardly conscious of where he was going. He pushed away the thoughts that came into his mind, and kept moving. He became aware of a slight sense of security as he turned into a lighted street where there were people and high buildings and blinking signs. After a while he found himself in the dim lobby of the structure that housed his office. Then he realised why he couldn't go home, why he daren't go home—after what had happened at the office of Dr Trevethick.

'Hello, Mr Wran,' said the night elevator man, a burly figure in overalls, sliding open the grille-work door to the old-fashioned cage. 'I didn't know you were working nights now, too.'

Catesby stepped in automatically. 'Sudden rush of orders,' he murmured inanely. 'Some stuff that has to be gotten out.'

The cage creaked to a stop at the top floor. 'Be working very late, Mr Wran?'

He nodded vaguely, watched the car slide out of sight, found his keys, swiftly crossed the outer office, and entered his own. His hand went out to the light switch, but then the thought occurred to him that the two lighted windows, standing out against the dark bulk of the building, would indicate his whereabouts and serve as a goal towards which something could crawl and climb. He moved his chair so that the back was against the wall and sat down in the semi-darkness. He did not remove his overcoat.

For a long time he sat there motionless, listening to his own breathing and the faraway sounds from the streets below: the thin metallic surge of the crosstown streetcar, the farther one of the elevated, faint lonely cries and honkings, indistinct rumblings. Words he had spoken to Miss Millick in nervous jest came back to him with the bitter taste of truth. He found himself unable to reason critically or connectedly, but by their own volition thoughts rose up into his mind and gyrated slowly and rearranged themselves with the inevitable movement of planets.

Gradually his mental picture of the world was transformed. No longer a world of material atoms and empty space, but a world in which the bodiless existed and moved according to its own obscure laws or unpredictable impulses. The new picture illuminated with dreadful clarity certain general facts which had always bewildered and troubled him and from which he had tried to hide; the inevitability of hate and war, the diabolically timed mischances which wreck the best of human intentions, the walls of wilful misunderstanding that divide one man from another, the eternal vitality of cruelty and ignorance and greed. They seemed appropriate now, necessary parts of the picture. And superstition only a kind of wisdom.

Then his thoughts returned to himself and the question he had asked Miss Millick, 'What would such a thing want from a person? Sacrifices? Worship. Or just fear? What could you do to stop it from troubling you?' It had become a practical question.

With an explosive jangle, the phone began to ring. 'Cate, I've been trying everywhere to get you,' said his wife. 'I never thought you'd be at the office. What are you doing? I've been worried.'

He said something about work.

'You'll be home right away?' came the faint anxious question. 'I'm a little frightened. Ronny just had a scare. It woke him up. He kept pointing to the window saying,

"Black man, black man." Of course it's something he dreamed. But I'm frightened. You will be home? What's that, dear? Can't you hear me?'

'I will. Right away,' he said. Then he was out of the office, buzzing the night bell and peering down the shaft.

He saw it peering up the shaft at him from the deep shadows three floors below, the sacking face pressed against the iron grille-work. It started up the stair at a shockingly swift, shambling gait, vanishing temporarily from sight as it swung into the second corridor below.

Catesby clawed at the door to the office, realised he had not locked it, pushed it in, slammed and locked it behind him, retreated to the other side of the room, cowered between the filing cases and the wall. His teeth were clicking. He heard the groan of the rising cage. A silhouette darkened the frosted glass of the door, blotting out part of the grotesque reverse of the company name. After a little the door opened.

The big-globed overhead light flared on and, standing inside the door, her hand on the switch, was Miss Millick.

'Why, Mr Wran,' she stammered vacuously. 'I didn't know you were here. I'd just come in to do some extra typing after the movie. I didn't . . . but the lights weren't on. What were you——'

He stared at her. He wanted to shout in relief, grab hold of her, talk rapidly. He realised he was grinning hysterically.

'Why, Mr Wran, what's happened to you?' she asked embarrassedly, ending with a stupid titter. 'Are you feeling sick? Isn't there something I can do for you?'

He shook his head jerkily and managed to say, 'No, I'm just leaving. I was doing some extra work myself.'

'But you *look* sick,' she insisted, and walked over towards him. He inconsequently realised she must have stepped in mud, for her high-heeled shoes left neat black prints.

'Yes, I'm sure you must be sick. You're so terribly pale.'

She sounded like an enthusiastic, incompetent nurse. Her face brightened with a sudden inspiration. 'I've got something in my bag, that'll fix you up right away,' she said. 'It's for indigestion.'

She fumbled at her stuffed oblong purse. He noticed that she was absent-mindedly holding it shut with one hand while she tried to open it with the other. Then, under his very eyes, he saw her bend back the thick prongs of metal locking the purse as if they were tinfoil, or as if her fingers had become a pair of steel pliers.

Instantly his memory recited the words he had spoken to Miss Millick that afternoon. 'It couldn't hurt you physically —at first . . . gradually get its hooks into the world . . . might even get control of suitably vacuous minds. Then it could hurt whomever it wanted.' A sickish, cold feeling grew inside him. He began to edge towards the door.

But Miss Millick hurried ahead of him.

'You don't have to wait, Fred,' she called. 'Mr Wran's decided to stay a while longer.'

The door of the cage shut with a mechanical rattle. The cage creaked. Then she turned around in the door.

'Why, Mr Wran,' she gurgled reproachfully. 'I just couldn't think of letting you go home now. I'm sure you're terribly unwell. Why, you might collapse in the street. You've just got to stay here until you feel different.'

The creaking died away. He stood in the centre of the office, motionless. His eyes traced the coal-black course of Miss Millick's footprints to where she stood blocking the door. Then a sound that was almost a scream was wrenched out of him, for it seemed to him that the blackness was creeping up her legs under the thin stockings.

'Why, Mr Wran,' she said, 'You're acting as if you were crazy. You must lie down for a while. Here, I'll help you off with your coat.'

The nauseously idiotic and rasping note was the same; only it had been intensified. As she came towards him he turned and ran through the storeroom, clattered a key desperately at the lock of the second door to the corridor.

'Why, Mr Wran,' he heard her call, 'are you having some kind of a fit? You must let me help you.'

The door came open and he plunged out into the corridor and up the stairs immediately ahead. It was only when he reached the top that he realised the heavy steel door in front of him led to the roof. He jerked up the catch.

'Why, Mr Wran, you mustn't run away. I'm coming after you.'

Then he was out on the gritty gravel of the roof. The night sky was clouded and murky, with a faint pinkish glow from the neon signs. From the distant mills rose a ghostly spurt of flame. He ran to the edge. The street lights glared dizzily upwards. Two men were tiny round blobs of hat and shoulders. He swung around.

The thing was in the doorway. The voice was no longer solicitous but moronically playful, each sentence ending in a titter.

'Why, Mr Wran, why have you come up here? We're all alone. Just think, I might push you off.'

The thing came slowly towards him. He moved backwards until his heel touched the low parapet. Without knowing why, or what he was going to do, he dropped to his knees. He dared not look at the face as it came nearer, a focus for the worst in the world, a gathering point for poisons from everywhere. Then the lucidity of terror took possession of his mind, and words formed on his lips.

'I will obey you. You are my god,' he said. 'You have supreme power over man and his animals and his machines. You rule this city and all others. I recognise that.'

Again the titter, closer. 'Why, Mr Wran, you never talked like this before. Do you mean it?'

'The world is yours to do with as you will, save or tear to pieces,' he answered fawningly, the words automatically fitting themselves together in vaguely liturgical patterns. 'I recognise that. I will praise, I will sacrifice. In smoke and soot I will worship you for ever.'

The voice did not answer. He looked up. There was only Miss Millick, deathly pale and swaying drunkenly. Her eyes were closed. He caught her as she wobbled towards him. His knees gave way under the added weight and they sank down together on the edge of the roof.

After a while she began to twitch. Small noises came from her throat and her eyelids edged open.

'Come on, we'll go downstairs,' he murmured jerkily, trying to draw her up. 'You're feeling bad.'

'I'm terribly dizzy,' she whispered. 'I must have fainted, I didn't eat enough. And then I'm so nervous lately, about the war and everything, I guess. Why, we're on the roof! Did you bring me up here to get some air? Or did I come up without knowing it? I'm awfully foolish. I used to walk in my sleep, my mother said.'

As he helped her down the stairs, she turned and looked at him. 'Why, Mr Wran,' she said, faintly, 'you've got a big black smudge on your forehead. Here, let me get it off for you.' Weakly she rubbed at it with her handkerchief. She started to sway again and he steadied her.

'No, I'll be all right,' she said. 'Only I feel cold. What happened, Mr Wran? Did I have some sort of fainting spell?'

He told her it was something like that.

Later, riding home in the empty elevated car, he wondered how long he would be safe from the thing. It was a purely practical problem. He had no way of knowing, but instinct told him he had satisfied the brute for some time. Would it want more when it came again? Time enough to answer that question when it arose. It might be hard, he realised, to keep out of an insane asylum. With Helen and Ronny to protect, as well as himself, he would have to be careful and tight-lipped. He began to speculate as to how many other men and women had seen the thing or things like it.

The elevated slowed and lurched in a familiar fashion. He looked at the roofs near the curve. They seemed very ordinary, as if what made them impressive had gone away for a while.

Aunt Jezebel's House

JOAN AIKEN

The last two stories in this collection are both about children and the supernatural. Child spirits, though recorded much less frequently than the spirits of men and women, do however feature from time to time in legends and are said to have the strongest emotional effect on those who see them. The first contributor is Joan Aiken, a superb creator of fantasy who writes for both adult and young readers. She is perhaps better equipped than many of her contemporaries, being the daughter of that master of the macabre, Conrad Aiken, and having grown up in a haunted house! Joan was born at Rye in Sussex and the family home was haunted by an old astrologer named Samuel Jeakes. This, combined with reading her father's chilling stories—including the classic "Mr. Arcularis"—prompted her to begin writing horror tales herself. (She actually began a Gothic novel called "Her Husband was a Demon" when she was barely a teenager.) Today, her reputation is international and her stories much anthologised. Yet here is a tale which she wrote at the age of 17 about her ghostly background, and which has not previously been published. In sending it to me for this book, Joan wrote, 'It relates in an oblique way to the haunted home of my childhood, and also embodies a story which did happen to someone I knew. My stepfather, Martin Armstrong (author of that horror classic, "The Pipe Smokers") often told this story of the small boy he had seen sitting in the train between Rye and Hastings, six inches above the seat, who then slowly vanished—and he was the most sceptical, un-supernatural person imaginable. So at the age of 17 I pinched this idea and wove it into a story—"Aunt Jezebel's House".' Although it is unmistakably the work of a youthful writer, I hope you will enjoy it as much as I did.

It was late autumn when Mr Wintergreen took his journey; a sad, gusty day, when cuttings from the trimmed hedges scuttered down the roads, and the country shivered and shrugged into itself in preparation for the winter. Mr Wintergreen knew nothing of this, for he slept in the train until he reached Hastings, and when, standing on the plat-form, he looked at his watch and discovered that he had half an hour to wait before the next train, he went straight into the waiting room, where there was a fire and some highly coloured posters of the South Coast. Here he sat, and tapped with some irritation on the arm of his chair. He had not yet learned how to do nothing.

Eventually the small train that was to take him to Rye appeared, and he settled himself into a corner seat and tried to sleep again. But sleep had deserted him, and as the train moved slowly out of the station, he found himself reviewing, in a brisk and slightly exasperating way, the chain of circumstances which had brought him here, to creep slowly along the local line, through the misty valleys and across the marsh from Hastings to Rye.

'It's thrown away on you, of course, that house,' his sister had said, when she had heard about it. The remark had annoyed him, and it was that which had really decided him to come.

'Why thrown away?' he demanded.

Maud had put down her knife and fork and gravely regarded him across the table.

'Because,' she said at length, 'you haven't an ounce of imagination. A nice villa in Pinner or Kingston would suit you just as well. Nor do I see any chance of your learning to appreciate it. A businessman you have been all your life and a businessman you will remain, however much you retire, and cast all that behind you, and try to live in Aunt Jezebel's house. It's wasted on you.'

'I don't know what you're talking about,' he said stiffly; 'I think I may say that I appreciate beautiful houses just as much as you do.'

Maud threw back her head and gave a short, derisive cough of laughter. 'A man who can make a remark like that . . .' she said, and then, more seriously, 'We won't argue about it. We should only go on all night, and I should never convince you, because you don't understand really what I mean.'

'Well, what *do* you mean?' he asked unreasonably.

'Oh well,' said Maud, considering him again, 'you'll miss such a lot. The house is haunted, of course, but you won't notice that. I expect you'll trample on the wretched ghosts, from sheer lack of observation. But it's not only that. The whole place is alive—crammed with things that you'll never see. Thank heaven Aunt Jezebel made the provision that you shouldn't alter the house at all.'

'Really, Maud,' he exclaimed crossly, 'I'm not such a vandal as you seem to be making out.'

Maud smiled at him oddly and said, 'Well, write and tell me if you've seen anything amusing when you've been in the house a month or so.'

'Amusing? What should I see?' he asked obstinately.

But Maud stood up and looked at her watch. 'I must go,' she said. 'It was nice seeing you, Harry, and I hope you enjoy yourself. Give my love to Aunt Jezebel's ghost if it has joined the others.'

She walked away, a tall, middle-aged woman with a ghost of malice in her eye, and he drew a breath of exasperation as he looked after. Because, really, though he was very fond of her, she did say the most fantastic things sometimes. And her insinuation that he couldn't appreciate Aunt Jezebel's house, and all that peculiar nonsense, was one of them. However, he would show her. Insensibly he had made up his mind, which had been uncertain before, not to let the house, but to go and live in it himself, at least for six months. Then he would see. Goodness knows what he would do with himself in Rye. Play golf, of course, and he believed there was a chess club. And the Madgewicks lived not far away in Iden. And he could have Maud and Hugh to stay over Christmas. Young Harry, too. Harry was his nephew, the son of Jack, who was killed in the Great War. He had been brought up principally by Aunt Jezebel, which accounted for his oddness. Not the sort of young man one could *like*, thought Mr Wintergreen, but still, he would probably enjoy spending Christmas in the old house, and it was really impossible not to ask him.

Harry had certainly taken the whole thing in a very peculiar way.

'Of course it's the chance of a lifetime, your going to live there,' he had said, looking at his uncle with the same considering expression which had been on Maud's face.

'Oh?' Mr Wintergreen had said.

'I envy you enormously,' Harry went on. 'Living in that house all alone, you ought to learn a lot.'

'*Learn* a lot?' The boy was really crazier than Maud. 'What do you expect me to learn?'

'Well, no, perhaps you won't,' said Harry. 'Perhaps you're

too thick-skinned. I think that it would need a considerable shock even to show you something that lay under your nose.'

This was hardly polite, and Mr Wintergreen told his nephew so.

'Possibly not,' Harry answered unabashed. 'But perfectly true. For instance—can you hear that?' With one hand on his uncle's arm he kept him still, and the other hand was raised in the air, pointing to nothing.

'Hear what?' Mr Wintergreen asked tartly, after two minutes of unfruitful silence.

'I told you so,' said Harry, and would explain himself no further. His uncle sighed with exasperation.

'I sometimes think, Harry,' he began, and then relapsed into silence. For after all, what did he think, except that Harry ought to go into some sensible profession, or alternatively into a lunatic asylum, instead of wasting his time painting pictures which didn't make sense.

'I know,' answered Harry, reading his thought. 'But you see, I was brought up in Aunt Jezebel's house, and that rather does away with one's sense of convention. Look at Aunt Jezebel.'

Mr Wintergreen preferred not to look at Aunt Jezebel, who had been a sore point with him. Why the old thing had chosen to leave him her house after years of icy silence between them, he could not imagine.

'It was her idea of a joke,' Maud had said once. Which didn't make sense. Yes, there was no doubt that Maud could be an irritating creature. He went over his conversation with her again, and was glad that he had decided to come to the house.

He would show the pair of them whether he could appreciate it or not. He was not quite sure how, but he would show them. He hoped that Mrs Fitch had lit the fires. It was going to be a cold evening.

While this train of thought had made its circuitous way through Mr Wintergreen's mind, he had been sitting and staring with an unseeing gaze at the other side of the railway carriage. Now he relaxed, and looked at the four people who were facing him. And gave a violent start. He had not seen anything surprising. It was simply that he had thought there were only three people on the opposite seat, and he now saw that there were four. The fourth was a small boy who was sitting between the large American lady and the sleeping vicar. Mr Wintergreen thought that he had been keeping that particular piece of space under a searching gaze for the last quarter of an hour, and that he would have noticed the boy get in at one of the halts they had passed. But evidently he had been too much absorbed in his thoughts to observe the entry of the child who confronted him, and who certainly had not been there when they left Hastings.

Oh well, he said to himself, what did it matter where he got in, whether at Doleham or Snailham? He turned and looked at the wide marsh, stretching away to the grey verge of the sea. But though his eye took in sheep and seagulls and the dusk, his mind, ill at ease, reverted to the boy and drew his head round to look again. Then he saw what his instinct had been trying to tell him. The small boy was dressed with extreme neatness in slightly old-fashioned clothes. He sat forward, very upright, with his knees together and his hands on them. He had a bright-eyed, alert face, and dark, unusually dark hair. He hardly looked English. There was an unusual expression on his face, too, which Mr Wintergreen tried to classify. It was not mischievous, nor amused, nor impudent. He decided that it was nothing more than an intensely alert, sparrowlike interest. The whole poise of him, the cock of his head, the placing of his hands, and knees drawn together, denoted an unblinking, watchful attention. These, though, were not the things that held Mr Wintergreen in a cold, fascinated grip, that dried the inside of his mouth and caused a strange, weak ache to take possession of the backs of his knees. The small boy had nothing more than the appearance of any other small boy, save that he was sitting on the air, six inches above the seat of the carriage.

No one else had noticed it. The vicar slept, the American lady was too occupied with her furs. The other people in the carriage were either asleep, or, Mr Wintergreen thought with a touch of superiority, remarkably unobservant.

His thoughts were diverted from the problem by the sudden stopping of the train somewhere outside Rye. The guard came in.

'The barrier is being repaired,' he said conversationally, 'can I see your tickets now, please?'

They shuffled in bags and pockets, and one by one produced their tickets. All except the small boy. When the guard looked at him he spread out his hands and said, politely, but firmly,

'I haf no ticket.'

'Why not?' asked the guard, assuming a stern voice. The boy looked at him inquiringly.

'How did you manage to get on the train without a ticket?' the guard repeated. 'Where did you get on?'

'I do not spik English well,' said the little boy, and looked appealingly round the carriage. The American woman took instant pity on him.

'I'll pay your fare,' she said with a large, protective gesture. 'Did he get on at the last stop? I didn't actually notice. Will that be all right, Inspector?' The guard seemed to think that it would be, and she bought him a ticket to Rye, where, apparently, he wanted to go. It was handed over, they settled down again, and the guard went away, giving the boy another firm look.

'Are you being met at Rye?' the American woman asked him. He shook his head.

'Well!' she exclaimed. 'Think of that! Will you be able to find your way? It'll be dark.' He shook his head again, doubtfully.

'I do not understand,' he said.

'Can you find your way to where you live? Are you staying in Rye?' she pressed him.

Another shake of his head. He seemed completely lost.

'Don't you know where you are staying?' she exclaimed. 'Look, you tell me the name, and I'll see you there.'

'Name?' he said. The whole carriage was listening by now.

'Yes, the name of the people you know in Rye. Is it your mother and father?'

'No. There is no one, thank you,' he said politely. She became more and more agitated, and went on questioning him. He answered, word by word. Mr Wintergreen stared once more at the vacant six inches between him and the seat and wondered if he was going mad.

'Well,' the American woman said finally, 'if you don't know where you have come from or where you are going, you're just staying with me for the night, and tomorrow we'll see.'

'Thank you,' the little boy said gravely.

'I shall certainly adopt him,' she said in a loud whisper to the rest of the carriage. 'Did you ever see anything so cute?'

'But—you *can't*!' Mr Wintergreen felt like shrieking. He kept quiet with an effort. The train started again. Could one prevent a wealthy American woman from adopting a small boy who didn't exist? She would think that he was mad, he told himself. The small boy sat looking about him more alertly than ever, and the train drew into the station. They all got out on to the dusky platform, and a spasm of courage came to him. He hurried to the side of the American woman and said in her ear,

'You can't possible think of adopting that small boy.'

'Why not?' she exclaimed, looking at him in astonishment. 'I think he's perfectly sweet. Gracious, you don't mean that you know anything bad about him, do you?'

'Of course not,' he replied testily. 'I never saw him in my life before. But look, my good woman, at the way he walks.'

For the small boy, crossing the line with the crowd, just

in front of them, was walking in the air six inches above the wooden boarding.

'Don't be ridiculous,' she said, staring at him, still more surprised. 'He walks very nicely. I can't think what you're talking about.'

'But can't you *see*?' he persisted madly. 'He's walking six inches above the ground.'

She gave him a horrified glance, shook off his arm, and moved hastily away. The two of them went off together among the crowd, she holding the little boy's hand, he sliding smoothly along on the air beside her.

Mr Wintergreen stood still in the station entrance and rubbed his forehead. Well, really, *what* could one believe? He was glad, very glad that Harry and Maud had not been there. They would have muddled him far worse than before, with their plausible, unreasonable explanations. As it was . . . he scratched his forehead again and stepped out, with a shade of hesitation, through the dim streets of Rye towards Aunt Jezebel's House.

Fever Dream

RAY BRADBURY

This last item is not really a ghost story although its inspiration was ghostly and there is certainly something very supernatural about what happens to the little boy who is the central character. It is, though, a very topical story, for it deals with the 'possession' of a human being—a subject that has hardly been out of the newspapers or off the television since it was highlighted in the film, The Exorcist. *The author, Ray Bradbury, sees possession for what it most certainly is, a disease or illness, and around that has woven a really frightening tale. Ray is, of course, very well known to enthusiasts of fantasy fiction, particularly those who have read my previous anthologies for they will know how highly I rate his unique imagination and magical prose. Born and brought up in the small town of Waukegan in*

Illinois, he had what he says can only be called a haunted childhood. 'When I lay in bed at night I heard ghosts in the attic and saw all sorts of strange things in my mind—I guess I was possessed by fantasy from an early age.' These influences are very evident in his stories, a good many of which feature small boys modelled on himself. The writing of them, too, can be very unusual. As he says, 'A weird feeling I get is that the words are flowing in from some clandestine and mysterious source outside of me. Many times I sit back, really astonished at what's on the paper.' The story here, "Fever Dream" combines all these elements of Ray's life, and may just be the strangest and most eerie story of the supernatural you'll ever read.

They put him between fresh, clean, laundered sheets and there was always a newly squeezed glass of thick orange juice on the table under the dim pink lamp. All Charles had to do was call and Mom or Dad would stick their heads into his room to see how sick he was. The acoustics of the room were fine; you could hear the toilet gargling its porcelain throat in the mornings, you could hear rain tap the roof or sly mice run in the secret walls, the canary singing in its cage downstairs. If you were very alert, sickness wasn't too bad.

He was fifteen, Charles was. It was mid September, with the land beginning to burn with autumn. He lay in the bed for three days before the terror overcame him.

His hand began to change. His right hand. He looked at it and it was hot and sweating there on the counterpane, alone. It fluttered, it moved a bit. Then it lay there, changing colour.

That afternoon the doctor came again and tapped his thin chest like a little drum. 'How are you?' asked the doctor, smiling. 'I know, don't tell me: "My *cold* is fine, Doctor, but I feel lousy!" Ha!' He laughed at his own oft-repeated joke.

Charles lay there and for him that terrible and ancient jest was becoming a reality. The joke fixed itself in his mind.

His mind touched and drew away from it in a pale terror. The doctor did not know how cruel he was with his jokes! 'Doctor,' whispered Charles, lying flat and colourless. 'My *hand*, it doesn't *belong* to me any more. This morning it *changed* into something else. I want you to change it back, Doctor, Doctor!'

The doctor showed his teeth and patted his hand. 'It looks fine to me, son. You just had a little fever dream.'

'But it changed, Doctor, oh, Doctor,' cried Charles, pitifully holding up his pale wild hand. 'It *did*!'

The doctor winked. 'I'll give you a pink pill for that.' He popped a tablet on to Charles's tongue. 'Swallow!'

'Will it make my hand change back and become *me*, again?'

'Yes, yes.'

The house was silent when the doctor drove off down the road in his carriage under the quiet, blue September sky. A clock ticked far below in the kitchen world. Charles lay looking at his hand.

It did not change back. It was still—something else.

The wind blew outside. Leaves fell against the cool window.

At four o'clock his other hand changed. It seemed almost to become a fever, a chemical, a virus. It pulsed and shifted, cell by cell. It beat like a warm heart. The fingernails turned blue and then red. It took about an hour for it to change and when it was finished, it looked just like any ordinary hand. But it was not ordinary. It no longer was him any more. He lay in a fascinated horror and then fell into an exhausted sleep.

Mother brought the soup up at six. He wouldn't touch it. 'I haven't any hands,' he said, eyes shut.

'Your hands are perfectly good,' said Mother.

'No,' he wailed. 'My hands are gone. I feel like I have stumps. Oh, Mama, Mama, hold me, hold me, I'm scared!'

She had to feed him herself.

'Mama,' he said, 'get the doctor, please, again, I'm so sick.'

'The doctor'll be here tonight at eight,' she said, and went out.

At seven, with night dark and close around the house, Charles was sitting up in bed when he felt the thing happening to first one leg then the other. 'Mama! Come quick!' he screamed.

But when Mama came the thing was no longer happening.

When she went downstairs, he simply lay without fighting as his legs beat and beat, grew warm, red hot, and the room filled with the warmth of his feverish change. The glow crept up from his toes to his ankles and then to his knees.

'May I come in?' The doctor smiled in the doorway.

'Doctor!' cried Charles. 'Hurry, take off my blankets!'

The doctor lifted the blankets tolerantly. 'There you are. Whole and healthy. Sweating, though. A little fever. I told you not to move around, bad boy.' He pinched the moist pink cheek. 'Did the pills help? Did your hand change back?'

'No, no, now it's my other hand and my legs!'

'Well, well, I'll have to give you three more pills, one for each limb, eh, my little peach?' laughed the doctor.

'Will they help me? Please, please. What've I *got*?'

'A mild case of scarlet fever, complicated by a slight cold.'

'Is it a germ that lives and has more little germs in me?'

'Yes.'

'Are you *sure* it's scarlet fever? You haven't taken any tests!'

'I guess I know a certain fever when I see one,' said the doctor, checking the boy's pulse with cool authority.

Charles lay there, not speaking until the doctor was crisply packing his black kit. Then in the silent room, the boy's voice made a small, weak pattern, his eyes alight with remembrance. 'I read a book once. About petrified trees, wood turning to stone. About how trees fell and rotted and minerals got in and built up and they look just like trees, but they're not, they're stone.' He stopped. In the quiet warm room his breathing sounded.

'Well?' asked the doctor.

'I've been thinking,' said Charles, after a time. 'Do germs ever get big? I mean in biology class they told us about one-celled animals, amoebas and things, and how, millions of years ago, they got together until there was a bunch and they made the first body. And more and more cells got together and got bigger and then finally maybe there was a fish and finally here *we* are, and all we are is a bunch of cells that decided to get together, to help each other out. Isn't that right?' Charles wet his feverish lips.

'What's all this about?' The doctor bent over him.

'I've got to tell you this. Doctor, oh, I've got to!' he cried. 'What would happen, oh just pretend, please pretend, that just like in the old days, a lot of microbes got together and wanted to make a bunch, and reproduced and made *more*——'

His white hands were on his chest now, crawling towards his throat.

'And they decided to *take over* a person!' cried Charles.

'Take over a person?'

'Yes, *become* a person. *Me*, my hands, my feet! What if a disease somehow knew how to kill a person and yet live after him?'

He screamed.

The hands were on his neck.

The doctor moved forward, shouting.

At nine o'clock the doctor was escorted out to his carriage by the mother and father, who handed him up his bag. They conversed in the cool night wind for a few minutes. 'Just be sure his hands are kept strapped to his legs,' said the doctor. 'I don't want him hurting himself!'

'Will he be all right, Doctor?' The mother held to his arm a moment.

He patted her shoulder. 'Haven't I been your family physician for thirty years? It's the fever, he imagines things.'

'But those bruises on his throat, he almost choked himself.'

'Just you keep him strapped; he'll be all right in the morning.'

The horse and carriage moved off down the dark September road.

At three in the morning, Charles was still awake in his small back room. The bed was damp under his head and his back. He was very warm. Now he no longer had any arms or legs, and his body was beginning to change. He did not move on the bed, but looked at the vast blank ceiling space with insane concentration. For a while he had screamed and thrashed but now he was weak and hoarse from it, and his mother had gotten up a number of times to soothe his brow with a wet towel. Now he was silent, his hands strapped to his legs.

He felt the walls of his body change, the organs shift, the lungs catch fire like burning bellows of pink alcohol. The room was lighted up as with the flickerings of a hearthplace.

Now he had no body. It was all gone. It was under him, but it was filled with a vast pulse of some burning, lethargic drug. It was as if a guillotine had neatly lopped off his head and his head lay shining on a midnight pillow while the body, below, still alive, belonged to somebody else. The disease had eaten his body and from the eating had reproduced itself in feverish duplicate. There were the little hand-hairs and the fingernails and the scars and the toenails and the tiny mole on his right hip, all done again in perfect fashion.

I am dead, he thought. I've been killed, and yet I live. My body is dead, it is all disease and nobody will know. I will walk around and it will not be me, it will be something else. It will be something all bad, all evil, so big and so evil it's hard to understand or think about. Something that will buy shoes and drink water and get married some day maybe and do more evil in the world than has ever been done.

Now the warmth was stealing up his neck, into his cheeks, like a hot wine. His lips burned, his eyelids, like leaves, caught fire. His nostrils breathed out blue flame, faintly, faintly.

This will be all, he thought. I'll take my head and my brain and fix each eye and every tooth and all the marks in my brain, and every hair and every wrinkle in my ears, and there'll be nothing left of me.

He felt his brain fill with a boiling mercury. He felt his left eye clench in upon itself and, like a snail, withdraw, shift. He was blind in his left eye. It no longer belonged to him. It was enemy territory. His tongue was gone, cut out. His left cheek was numbed, lost. His left ear stopped hearing. It belonged to someone else now. This thing that was being born, this mineral thing replacing the wooden log, this disease replacing healthy animal cell.

He tried to scream and he was able to scream loud and high and sharply in the room, just as his brain flooded down, his right eye and right ear were cut out, he was blind and deaf, all fire and terror, all panic, all death.

His scream stopped before his mother ran through the door to his side.

It was a good, clear morning, with a brisk wind that helped carry doctor, horse and carriage along the road to halt before the house. In the window above, the boy stood, fully dressed. He did not wave when the doctor waved and called, 'What's this? Up? My God!'

The doctor almost ran upstairs. He came gasping into the bedroom.

'What are you doing out of bed?' he demanded of the boy. He tapped his thin chest, took his pulse and temperature. 'Absolutely amazing! Normal. Normal, by God!'

'I shall never be sick again in my life,' declared the boy, quietly, standing there, looking out of the wide window. 'Never.'

'I hope not. Why, you're looking fine, Charles.'

'Doctor?'

'Yes, Charles?'

'Can I go to school *now*?' asked Charles.

'Tomorrow will be time enough. You sound positively eager.'

'I am. I like school. All the kids. I want to play with them and wrestle with them, and spit on them and play with the girls' pigtails and shake the teacher's hand, and rub my hands on all the cloaks in the cloakroom, and I want to grow up and travel and shake hands with people all over the world, and be married and have lots of children, and go to libraries and handle books and—*all* of that I want to!' said the boy, looking off into the September morning. 'What's the name you called me?'

'What?' The doctor puzzled. 'I called you nothing but Charles.'

'It's better than no name at all, I guess,' Charles shrugged.

'I'm glad you want to go back to school,' said the doctor.

'I really anticipate it,' smiled the boy. 'Thank you for your help, Doctor. Shake hands.'

'Glad to.'

They shook hands gravely, and the clear wind blew through the open window. They shook hands for almost a minute, the boy smiling up at the old man and thanking him.

Then, laughing, the boy raced the doctor downstairs and out to his carriage. His mother and father followed for the happy farewell.

'Fit as a fiddle!' said the doctor. 'Incredible!'

'And strong,' said the father. 'He got out of his straps himself during the night. Didn't you, Charles?'

'Did I?' said the boy.

'You did! How?'

'Oh,' the boy said, 'that was a long time ago.'

'A long time ago!'

They all laughed, and while they were laughing, the quiet boy moved his bare foot on the pavement and brushed against a number of red ants that were scurrying about on the pavement. Secretly, his eyes shining, while his parents chatted with the old man, he saw the ants hesitate, quiver, and lie still on the cement. He knew they were cold now.

'Good-bye!'

The doctor drove away, waving.

The boy walked ahead of his parents. As he walked he looked away towards the town and began to hum 'School Days' under his breath.

'It's good to have him well again,' said the father.

'Listen to him. He's so looking forward to school!'

The boy turned quietly. He gave each of his parents a crushing hug. He kissed them both several times.

Then, without a word, he bounded up the steps into the house.

In the parlour, before the others entered, he quickly opened the birdcage, thrust his hand in, and petted the yellow canary, *once*.

Then he shut the cage door, stood back, and waited.

SC

The Ghost's companion